SCHEMING SPHYNX

PET WHISPERER P.I.
BOOK 16

MOLLY FITZ

ABOUT THIS BOOK

It all started when a vengeful seagull with a shady past promised to wage a brutal war against my wedding day. Things snowballed pretty quickly from there.

I always thought my special day would be perfect. Now, all I want is to get through it without any major catastrophes.

And that's pretty hard with four hyped-up cats running underfoot—two who are so desperately in love it makes you want to puke, and two more who very much don't want me as their new stepmother and aren't afraid to tell me so... constantly.

By the time a certain friend shows up with the film crew for her floundering reality TV in tow, I know I'm in big trouble.

Not only could I fail to make it down the aisle, but I also risk exposing my biggest, most intimate secret.

So when all is finally said and done, will I be saying "I do" to the man of my dreams or admitting "I can" when forced to confess to my Pet Whisperer abilities?

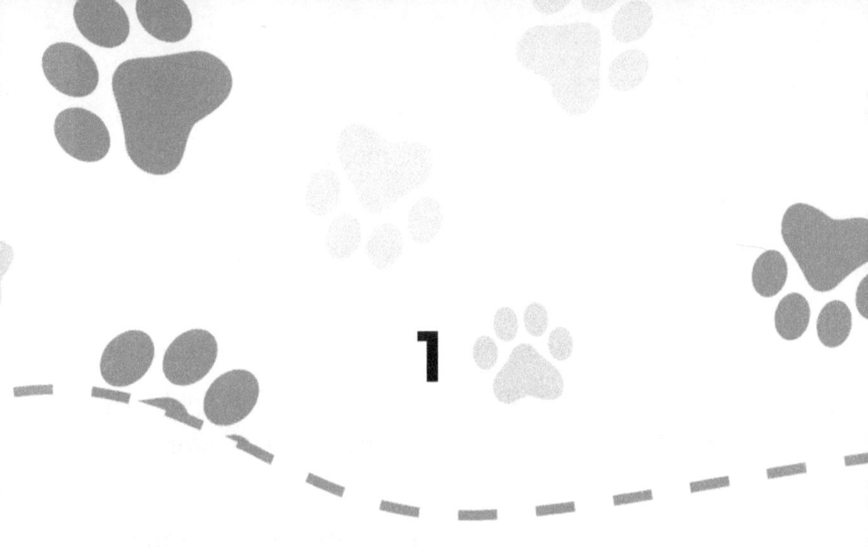

1

My name is Angie Russo, and in just a few short days, I will become Mrs. Charles Longfellow, III. It seems like it's been ages since that first day our eyes met across the office and I instantly fell head over heels for the handsome new law associate from California. Really, though, it's only been a couple years since that fateful day.

And even though I immediately fell in love, it took Charles a little longer to figure out I was the one he'd spend the rest of his life with. It all started when he blackmailed me into helping with a difficult double homicide case. He was the second person to learn of my strange ability to talk to animals—even I was still getting the hang of it then

—and rather than gawk at me, he decided to put me to work.

Now we've solved many cases, both together and apart, and in the process we've fallen incredibly and irrevocably in love. He's now the sole partner at the firm, and I've moved on from being a paralegal to working as a full-time private investigator... in theory.

In reality, I primarily live off my cat's trust fund, but I do try my best to find new mysteries to solve, whether or not my help has been requested. Why, just this spring, I solved the murder of my next-door neighbor. Oh, was that one a doozy!

Luckily, we've been light on work in the weeks that followed, giving me plenty of time to focus on wedding planning.

So, that's me. Former paralegal, current private investigator, future bride. Oh, you wanted to know more about the whole talking to animals thing?

Well, it all started when I met Octo-Cat at a rather unusual will reading. This was before Charles had even joined the firm. He was the first one to really trust me to help research our cases. Before that, I was mostly a glorified secretary. And that day, it was my job to make the coffee. Things didn't exactly go well, and let's just say I've had a completely rational fear of that particular appliance ever since.

The unexpected zap messed with something in my brain, and when I regained consciousness, I was met with big amber eyes and stinky tuna breath. Yes, the estate's primary beneficiary was a cat, and when he realized I could understand everything he was saying, he recruited me to help solve his owner's murder.

And thus a lifelong *something* was born. Most days Octo-Cat and I get along just fine, but sometimes he can be a real stinker. Still, I wouldn't trade him—or really any part of my life—for the world.

My true best friend is my nan. She's the main one who raised me while my parents focused on making the most of their careers. She's not even my biological grandmother, a fact I discovered only recently. And after months of searching and with a little help from a militant flock of seagulls, I was finally able to meet my Grandma Lyn—the one who gave birth to Mom.

Both will be at the wedding, which will definitely be awkward. But we'll have lots of other guests to help keep the two apart as much as possible.

Nan's dog Paisley, a mostly black tricolor

Chihuahua she rescued from the pound, is going to be the flower girl at our wedding. Pringle, the raccoon who lives in a treehouse in my backyard, is not invited but will probably crash the party anyway. Our seagull friends Bravo and Abigull have told us they'll be watching from the trees.

Another seagull I know, Alpha, has threatened to ruin the whole affair. He's also recently befriended Pringle and encouraged him to take part in a twelve-step program to help with his behavioral issues. I'm not sure I trust his motives on that one, but the group therapy has definitely been helping Pringle turn over a new leaf.

He's still not invited to the wedding, though.

I'll be plenty busy hosting all the guests we have coming from out of town. Even my old frenemy Bethany Peters is coming up from Georgia along with my cousin Mags to take part in the happiest day of my life to date.

Charles's family is coming out from California, of course, and our friend Sharon is taking a detour on her RV tour of the country to swing on by too. Basically, everyone who's anyone to us will be in attendance—past clients, old friends, distant family... Even my cat's girlfriend's owner is coming all the way from Colorado to offer her well wishes.

In lieu of a bridal party, our three cats will be standing at the altar with us. I've found adorable bowties for Octo-Cat and Jacques and a miniature lace veil for Jillianne. Charles hasn't been owned by cats as long as I have, but he's a sucker for the two hairless sphynxes he inherited from my first dead next-door neighbor, Senator Harlowe.

Over the last several months, I've been giving the two naked felines speech lessons to help them overcome their strange accents—not out of the goodness of my heart, but rather at Octo-Cat's demand. He made it very clear that neither Charles nor his cats would be welcome in our house unless the two kittyfolk stopped communicating in only riddles and rhymes.

It was a tall order, but I'm fairly accustomed to my cat bossing me around, and this demand wasn't particularly unreasonable as far as Octo-Cat goes, which meant I was happy to comply. Plus it gave me a chance to bond with Jacques and Jillianne ahead of us becoming one big happy family.

They weren't too sure about me at first, but now I'm fairly certain I've won them over... At least, I hope I have.

. . .

"Did you pick up my veil from the dry cleaner?" I bellowed at Nan as I rushed down the stairs to answer the door.

"On my list for this afternoon!" Nan shouted back as I flung open the door to reveal a massive pink balloon, which immediately floated forward and bopped me in the face.

"Oof, sorry. That one got away from me." The helium wrangler groaned while hanging on to the rest of his floating bouquet with two firm hands. "Where do you want them?"

"Out back. Let me show you."

As soon as the balloon vendor stepped back, I rushed out onto the porch and down the steps, realizing too late that I'd forgotten to put on any kind of slippers. The cold morning dew tickled my toes and made me shiver, but I was a woman on a mission.

T minus twenty-eight hours until the big *I do*. And I refused to let anyone stand in the way of me and my future husband, least of all some pesky seagull who had vowed to get his revenge on me— even though he was the one who'd ruined his flock; I'd simply uncovered the truth.

That's why, in lieu of flowers, I'd decided to decorate the backyard with hundreds and hundreds of balloons floating in the sky and forming an overhead canopy. That should keep any unwanted avian company away, or at least that was my hope.

"Isn't your wedding tomorrow?" the balloon guy asked as he affixed the balloons to the spot on the massive metal frame I'd just pointed out. "If we get some bad weather in, these will be ruined."

"No, that won't happen." I laughed under my breath. "I've already decided that the weather will be perfect both today and tomorrow."

"But you can't control the—"

"I've already decided that it will be fine," I said, biting off each word as I spoke it. I'd tried to arrange for the balloon canopy to be erected on the morning of the wedding but couldn't find a vendor who could work with that proposed schedule. Setting up a day early was the only choice I could make, since I refused to push the wedding back—not when I'd already waited this long to become Mrs. Charles Longfellow, III, now and forevermore.

"If you say so." He shrugged and got back to work. So much for *the customer is always right*.

I wrung my hands but somehow managed to hold my tongue. I wasn't usually so high-strung, but this was my wedding. It was the one day I needed to go perfectly right, and I already had at least one strike against me, seeing as a certain murderous seagull has threatened to upend the whole thing.

If I could just control the rest…

If I could just prevent anything else from going wrong…

Oops. I should have definitely known better than to tempt fate. As soon as I rounded the house, I saw two giant RVs sidling up my driveway.

And I already knew that whatever news they brought couldn't be good.

2

watched in horror as the RVs parked and half a dozen men scrambled out from the rear vehicle, holding a variety of boom mics, cameras, and other assorted film equipment.

"Excuse me!" I called, wrapping my arms around myself to stave off the early morning cold. I was still barefoot, which didn't help. "Excuse me! What are you doing?"

"Shhh, we're about to start filming," one of the men hissed in my direction before turning back to his team. "And in three... two... one... go."

That's when the door of the front RV flung open to reveal my friend Sharon carrying her white, long-haired cat Chester in her arms. "Oh, what a beautiful day for a wedding!" she exclaimed as the flowing fabric of her princess-cut evening gown swished around her ankles. "Don't you think so, Chessy?"

The group of men moved around her before one yelled, "Cut!"

"I think there might be some confusion. The wedding's tomorrow," I called helplessly as Sharon set her cat down and rushed over to envelop me in a giant bear hug.

"Oh, I know. We all know that. But it takes work to get the right shots, so we figured we'd show up a day early to make sure we get it all on camera. Thank you again for agreeing to this. It will be the perfect finale to the first season of Chessy's reality TV show."

My jaw dropped and practically hit the ground. "I didn't—I mean, I don't— Come again now?"

She lifted what appeared to be a freshly manicured hand to her chest in shock. "Why, it was on my RSVP card. Didn't you receive it?"

"You RSVPed with a plus-one," I ground out, trying so hard not to show my anger in that moment.

"And then I wrote the letters *R* and *V*. Sharon plus one extra RV. Our film crew." Upon finishing her asinine explanation, her face suddenly crumpled at the corners. "We're not unwelcome, are we? I've been talking this wedding up for the last several episodes. It would be a lot of work to remove all that, and then we'd have to come up with a different idea for the finale and everything. If our finale doesn't land just right, we may not be asked to renew for a second season, and we can't have that. Chessy is far too used to the glitz and glamour of celebrity life now. Besides, you knew I'd be filming through the end of June, so I just assumed an invite for me was an invite for the whole crew."

Well, now what in the heck was I supposed to do with all that?

"There'll be a handsome stipend for you, of course. In fact, the producers want to pay for your big day in its entirety."

I gulped down my anxiety and forced a smile. "Sharon, that's wonderful. Thank you," I said, even though I now had one more massive thing to worry about. Forget about ruining the day. If the camera crew caught me at the exact wrong moment, my little secret could be exposed for all of America to see. And that would ruin my entire life.

Yes, I had no doubts that if anyone beyond my very tight inner circle found out about my strange ability to talk with animals, my life would be ruined. No one would ever let me live normally again, and that's not the future I wanted to envision on this, the morning before my wedding.

"What's with the circus?" my cat asked, appearing suddenly behind me thanks to the electronic pet flap on the porch.

I pressed my lips in a straight line, unable to answer without risking a full revelation.

Sharon, of course, wasted no time scooping him up into her thick arms. "Oh, Tubby Tabby! It's so good to see you."

Octo-Cat's eyes widened in horror as our visitor brought her face closer and closer and then placed a kiss smack dab on his whiskered face.

"I will never forgive you for this, Angela. Never," he hissed before taking a swipe at Sharon and then wriggling free and racing back inside.

At this point, I had at least one hundred such threats of him withholding forgiveness into eternity, so I wasn't too worried about this one. Sharon's early arrival with her cinematographers, on the other hand? Definitely a very big problem.

I stared at the ground, doing my best to tune everything out as I thought quickly. "I still have a lot to do over the next..." I twisted my arm to glance at my smart watch. "Twenty-seven hours and eighteen minutes," I announced with a grimace, letting my arm fall back to my side.

"Say no more," Sharon crooned. "Chessy and I are happy to help."

"Actually." I paused to clear my throat. "Actually, it will be easier if I just do it myself. I'm sorry. It's just I have every single minute planned right until the main event. You're welcome to hang out and help Nan while your crew gets their shots, though. In fact, I'm sure she'd be happy for the company. C'mon, I'll take you to her now."

Sharon offered a sad smile that quickly morphed into a huge beaming grin. "I'd love to meet her, and I'd love it even more to have her all to myself. Lead the way." She motioned with a big sweeping gesture, then brought her hands up to pat down the sides of her blonde pixie cut and make sure it was all in place. "I will have to get some shots with Chessy when the crew is done getting their B-footage, but I made sure to get myself ready before we even arrived."

I nodded my approval as I led my overly punctual guest up the porch steps. "You look very nice. Hey, maybe you can show Nan how to make your famous lingonberry pie. She's a baker too, you know."

Sharon's brows furrowed as she shook her head emphatically. "Oh, no, no, no. It just wasn't the same after it cost that Junetta her life. Sure, it wasn't my fault, but well, her death sort of tainted the whole thing, if you know what I mean."

I definitely understood and respected her reasoning on that one, but I didn't really have time to help her and Nan find common ground beyond that. I was already behind schedule as it was.

Thankfully my grandmother was right where I left her, and a few moments later, Sharon and I found her bustling about the kitchen, doing who-knows-what. "Nan, Sharon. Sharon, Nan," I said before running back outside to lay down the law with the newly arrived film crew. Maybe I was becoming something of a bridezilla, but this was a pretty huge surprise to levy on someone right before her big day. A part of me wondered if my avian enemy Alpha had anything to do with the unplanned arrival, but I quickly brushed that concern aside.

Apart from me, the only person I knew who could speak with animals was my long-lost Grandma Lyn. Now that I thought about it, she would be here any minute too. I'd definitely need to pull her aside and explain our heightened risk of discovery. In fact...

I grabbed my cell phone from my jeans pocket and attempted to give my second grandmother a call. No such luck. She was probably already en route, which meant I needed to be extra vigilant.

Suddenly, a hurricane of horrid what-if scenarios swept into my brain, threatening to destroy everything in its path. I stood immobilized as scene by scene of probable mishaps played before my eyes. This was not good. Not good at all.

In fact, was it too late for the groom and I to elope?

Maybe I should give Charles a call and—

"Miss, Miss."

I was shaken from my stupor by the return of the balloon wrangler.

"I'm back with another batch. Is everything all right?"

"It's going to be fine," I reminded him, hating how enraged my usually perky voice sounded. "It's all going to be fine."

He nodded and backed away slowly, then took off to the backyard in a jerky power walk. I'd have laughed if I weren't already about to cry.

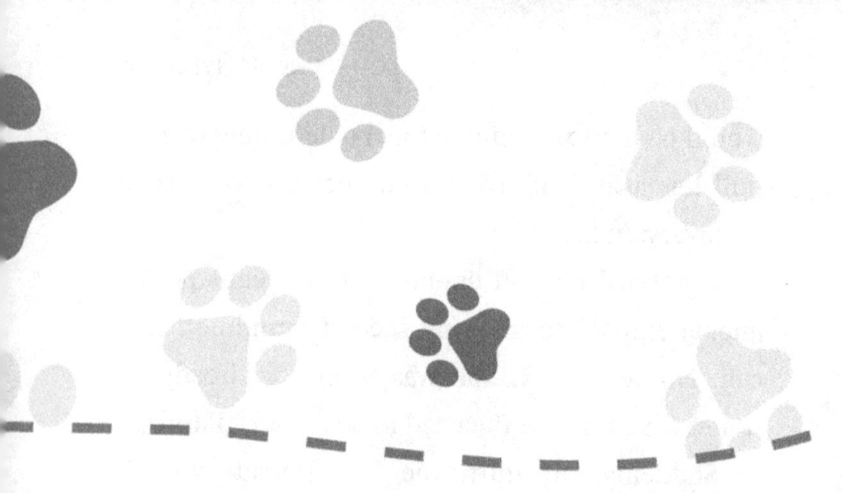

3

As I was putting the finishing touches on the seating arrangements for our reception, a soft knock sounded at the door. Nan and Sharon had left to run some errands near an hour ago, which meant it was up to me to answer the unexpected knock.

I tugged the door open to reveal… no one.

Odd.

With a shrug, I began to close the door again, but a small voice stopped me.

"Excuse me. I was hoping we could talk, please, if you don't mind."

Pringle the raccoon stood on his hind legs, clutching a tiny envelope between his clawed fingers. I wasn't yet used to him being polite, but ever since he'd joined AA—yes, Alcoholics Anonymous—he'd really turned over a new leaf. I loved that he was following the twelve-step program to overcome his obsessive and often hurtful behavior, even though I felt quite certain the little creature had never touched a drop of liquor his entire life.

What worried me, though, was the fact that a certain militant seagull had turned him on to the idea, and since I knew that Alpha's revenge would find me at any moment, I'd become suspicious of everything my raccoon neighbor said and did.

Then I remembered that I had one more reason to worry—there was a camera crew currently filming in my yard.

I stepped out onto the porch and glanced every which way to ensure no one saw what I was about to do. When I was satisfied I had a moment's privacy, I pulled Pringle into the house and shut the door behind us.

He immediately turned back. "Oh, no. I am not allowed in the house. If you ever catch me in here again, you're going to turn me into Davey Crockett memorabilia, and I don't think I'd like being a hat."

My chest tightened with guilt. To be fair, I'd made that threat after he kidnapped Nan's Chihuahua, carried her up to his tree fort, and locked her in a live trap as part of his imaginary gumshoe game.

"It's okay when you're invited," I said with what I hoped was a beatific smile.

"Thank you. I shall remember that," the raccoon answered, so unlike his usual self I had to wonder if this was an authentic change or just another one of his role-playing antics.

Pringle bowed, then held up the card he'd brought with him using both hands.

I plucked it from his fingers and examined both sides. It was one of the RSVP cards Charles and I had sent out with the wedding invitations. Each of the meal options was checked off, and a giant muddy paw print filled the left half of the card.

"My invite never arrived, so I figured it must have gotten lost in the mail. I didn't want to bother you, so I waited until I could find a blank one in the trash, and then I filled it out so that you would know I'm coming. I would never miss your big day, Miss Angela."

Sometimes this little trash panda really caught me off guard. I hadn't sent him an invite because he's a raccoon who lives in the treehouse in my backyard—and also because I strongly suspected Alpha would use him in his plot to ruin the whole thing. Still, my heart went out to him. God help him, he was trying very hard to be a good raccoon these days.

"Thank you, Pringle, that's very kind. I see here you will be having the chicken, fish, *and* vegetarian options for your dinner."

His smile widened, showing off those sharp little incisors. "Yes, you planned a perfect menu. I didn't want to miss out on any of it."

I chuckled to myself rather than point out the whole point of having options is that so guests could pick the one thing they liked best.

"Angela!" my cat's panicked cry sounded from the kitchen. "Angela, come here right now!"

Pringle offered me a knowing smile. "Duty calls, I see. If you'll just open the door, I'll see myself out."

I nodded and followed his instruction just as my frantic tabby bellowed my name once more. "Ange-laaaaaaaa!"

"I'm coming, I'm coming," I yelled, moving as quick as I could in his direction.

"What are these vulgar creatures doing drinking from *my* teacup? And eating *my* food?" he demanded, his tail flicking wildly behind him as he stared in horror at our two kitty guests.

"You remember Jacques and Jillianne," I said, reaching down to pet each of Charles's sphynx cats between their giant bat-like ears.

"Yes, I remember them, which is precisely why I don't want them here," Octo-Cat answered with a sneer.

"I don't like him staring while we're trying to have a meal," Jacques, the smaller sphynx, said with a huff.

"I don't like him in the same room as us at all," Jillianne, his large black companion, added.

"And I don't like them intruding in my home and then acting like I'm not even here!" Octo-Cat shouted right back, the fur on his spine now raised in aggression.

Well, this was not good. One of Nan's errands had involved picking up Charles's cats and bringing them here so they had some time to settle in before tomorrow's ceremony. Seeing as I'd been so immersed in my own to-do list, I hadn't realized she'd already deposited the two naked felines in our home—their home now, too, since Charles would be moving in, effective tomorrow.

"C'mon, Octo-Cat. I'll get you set up with fresh food and water in your bedroom."

His jaw dropped comically low. I swear it practically scraped the linoleum floor. "Me? You're forcing me to move? Why not them? Need I remind you, this is my house?"

"You know that Jacques and Jillianne will be living here now that Charles and I are getting married. None of this should be a surprise. You know—"

"I don't like his tone," one of the nudist cats interrupted.

"I don't like this place," the other added, and they both shuddered in eerie unison. "I don't like it at all."

It was fantastic that the sphynxes were no longer speaking strictly in rhymes and riddles. If only they hadn't instead defaulted to complaints as their primary method of communication. The two of them were dead ringers for Veruca Salt from *Charlie and the Chocolate Factory* these days, and I did not much care for that.

I turned away from J and J and focused my attention on Octo-Cat. He was rarely reasonable, but I had a better chance of getting through to him than my new step-cats—and here I thought our relationship had been progressing so nicely. "You have to be the one to go because you have your own bedroom that's set up perfectly to your liking. I realize you don't like the idea of sharing the house with other cats, but there's not really anything we can do about that."

The tabby gasped in horror. "You could not marry Up-Chuck for starters, or we could send those two interlopers to the animal rescue."

"Well, now you're definitely going to your room. You're being very rude to your new siblings and need a time-out." Having said my part, I did the thing my cat liked least. I hoisted him into my arms and carried him up the stairs straight to his bedroom.

"You can come out after you've had some time to think about what you've done," I said, blocking the door so he couldn't run out and end his punishment ahead of schedule.

He chuffed at this. "I've already thought about it, and I still one hundred percent agree with—"

I closed the door between us, not having the time to listen to his spoiled rant. I could hardly take one cat complaining at me day in and day out. How on earth was I going to handle three?

# 4

ake that four, four complaining cats all under one roof on the day before my nuptials.

Because less than an hour later, Christine arrived from Colorado with Octo-Cat's girlfriend Grizabella in hand. Oh why did I have to invite everyone to stay at my place while they were in town?

True, I've got the space in my giant manor home, but the added complications of catering to all my out-of-town arrivals were not helping with my state of mind. At least having Grizabella there would help to calm Octo-Cat, or so I hoped.

"Come in, come in," I cooed to Christine, giving her a quick hug before practically pushing her toward the staircase. "You two will stay in Octo-Cat's room. Let me show you where that is." Usually I called it the "fish tank" room when talking to outsiders, but if anyone would understand my cat having his own bedroom, it was the show queen Christine and her retired prize Himalayan.

"I'm rather tired from all the travel," the gorgeous new feline arrival explained around a yawn. "Be a dear and fetch my brush. Not the one with the steel bristles. The natural wood, darling. Oh, I must look a wreck. What will my hunka-burning kitty love think of me in this state?"

Clearly my cat was beginning to rub off on her, because otherwise such a refined purebred like Grizabella never would have uttered "hunka-burning kitty love."

Anyway, no time to puzzle over that. I still had a to-do list a million miles long. So I stuffed the two new arrivals into the bedroom, reminding Christine not to admit the two sphynx cats under any circumstances, then ran back downstairs to my post. I'd done my best to stagger everyone's arrivals, but some flights had been delayed whereas others seemed to be arriving early. Definitely not helpful.

Another knock at the door revealed the return of the balloon vendor. "I'm all set back there."

"Great, thanks." I offered him a kindly smile and then shut the door.

He knocked again.

"Yes?" I demanded, perhaps a bit hurried but not unkind.

He took off his hat and wrung it in his hands. "It's just that you said you'd write me a check once setup was complete, and I'd like to avoid another trip out if I can."

"Oh, right, yes, yes. Give me five minutes, and I'll be right back with your payment." I shut the door again and jogged up the stairs toward my office where I kept my checkbook locked in the top drawer of my desk. You can never be too careful, after all.

Christine intercepted me in the hallway. "Angie, do you have any clean towels? I'd love to grab a quick rinse. Wash that plane stink off me, you know?"

"Yes, of course. How are the cats getting on?" I turned on heel to face her, which set me slightly off balance. Luckily, the wall was there to help steady me.

Christine laughed and rolled her eyes as she

followed me toward the linen closet. "They haven't stopped grooming each other for even a second. I'm worried they won't be able to breathe!"

I chuckled, happy for them but also happy that I didn't have to watch their over-the-top display of affection. "Here are two towels and a washcloth. Bathroom's fourth door on the right. Need anything else while you have me?"

"A bottle of water?" Christine squeaked as if asking for this small allowance made her nervous.

I bobbed my head enthusiastically. "Yes, yes, be right back."

"You can just show me where it is. I'm happy to grab it myself. I know you're busy."

"Nonsense, you're my guest. I'll just run down and get you a couple bottles from the pantry and leave them in your room for when you're done with your shower, okay?"

I chugged down the stairs again, my breathing becoming labored as I ran up and down and all around this place. On my return trip up the stairs, my cell phone jangled in my pocket.

I fumbled the water bottles in my rush to answer. "How's my bride to be?" Charles crooned in that lovey-dovey voice of his that has a way of making my knees go week.

"Better now that I'm talking to you," I gushed right back, ignoring the feline lovers as I set the water bottles on the nightstand for Christine and then closed the door firmly behind me once again.

He sighed, and I couldn't tell whether it was swoony or sleepy. His words cleared that right up for me, however. "You sound a bit out of breath. I wish you'd let me come over and help with all these last-minute preparations."

He was right. I was exhausted to the max, but I refused to waste even a second, knowing that everything I was doing now would help form the perfect lifelong memory for the both of us.

Still, I could take a few minutes out of my busy schedule to chat with my fiancé. Couldn't I?

I clomped up the stairs to my tower bedroom, hoping I could get some privacy there. "You know how traditional your parents are. They're not even arriving until tomorrow morning, because they don't want to risk seeing me before the big reveal. Your mother would lose her mind if she knew you got a sneak peek."

"She doesn't have to know," he teased, and I could just picture the mischievous smile stretching across his face.

"Ah, ah, ah," I warned playfully. "Mama

Longfellow was very clear. We're not allowed to see each other for a full week before the wedding. That's the only way we can ensure a happy marriage. Don't you want a happy marriage, Charles?"

"I want my Angie," he said with a long-winded sigh. "I miss you."

"I miss you too. I love y—"

My phone began to beep, cutting me off. "Shoot. I'm getting another call. I have to go. Love you!"

"Hello?" a muffled voice rose from the other end of the line. It was vaguely familiar, but not one I could immediately place. "Angie?"

"Yes, hi. What's up?" I asked casually as my nerves once again began to fray.

"This is Reverend Stonehill. I'm so sorry to do this last minute, but I have an out-of-state family emergency, and well..."

I sucked in a deep breath, knowing what was coming next. "I'm not going to be able to officiate at your wedding tomorrow."

I held back tears and bobbed my head, using the repetitive motion to comfort me in this moment of despair. Reverend Stonehill was a man of God, and I knew he wouldn't lie to me. I also knew he wouldn't cancel without a really good reason.

Whatever he had going on must have been infinitely more important and more time-sensitive than my ceremony.

"I understand," I said, working hard to keep my voice from shaking, my tears from falling. "Thank you for letting me know." After a brief pause, I decided to add, "I will pray that your emergency works itself out soon." It seemed like the right thing to say, given the situation and the person I was talking to.

We said a quick goodbye, and then I fell back on my bed, letting the tears fall in waves. Soon I'd need to put on a happy face and help my next visitor get settled in, but before that happened, I just needed to let it all out. I tried to picture my tears as a poison being purged from my body so it couldn't hurt me anymore. But not even that helped.

Just one more day, I reminded myself yet again.

One more day to forever. Now it was like a meditative chant.

Instead of *om, om,* I kept telling myself *one, one.*

Just one more day to go, then my happily ever after would begin...

5

A soft scratching at my door pulled me from my woeful funk. "Paisley?" I called as I pushed myself to my feet and padded over to the door. I knew for a fact Octo-Cat was shut in his room, so it had to be our other furry roommate. I hadn't seen Paisley much that day, but her special brand of optimistic enthusiasm was just what I needed to start feeling better so I could get back to work.

But no, Nan's sweet little dog must have gone with her on errands, because Paisley wasn't the one waiting outside my door. It wasn't Octo-Cat, either. My actual visitors were far, far worse.

"I don't like it when she assumes we are a flea-ridden dog!" Jillianne said by way of hello. I was just about to defend Paisley's good, flee-free name when Jacques chimed in with, "I don't like when she closes doors and impedes our access. This is supposed to be our house now."

I bit back a sigh. Step or not, these sphynxes were my cat kids now. I had to make an effort to improve our relationship, no matter how much their complaints grated on me.

So I clasped my hands together and forced a smile. "Jacques and Jillianne, what can I do for you?"

"I don't like being bored," Jacques said with a groan.

"I don't like being cold," his sister added, and on they went with their litany of complaints.

"I don't like being hungry."

"I don't like how this place smells."

"I don't like how—"

"Okay, enough! What *do* you even actually like? Can we focus on that for a second please? I'm happy to help you, but you need to be a bit more specific—and also a bit nicer to me, please. We're family now, got it?"

The two cats sat in unified silence, staring up at

me with large unblinking eyes. I stared right back, unsure exactly what game we were playing but also knowing I couldn't afford to lose.

After at least two tense minutes, they turned tail and jogged back down the stairs.

"I don't like her," they agreed in perfect sync. Well, wasn't that just perfect?

I waited to make sure they had gotten to wherever they were going, then descended the stairs myself. I was already way behind on my schedule, thanks to my minor breakdown. I really needed to get back on track. First I would—

"Angelaaaaaa!" my cat called as I passed his bedroom door. Oh, good gravy. More cat drama? Wasn't I the lucky one?

I briefly contemplated ignoring the tabby, but then he added, "I know you're out there, and I know you can hear me. Now come in here. We have something important to discuss."

I hung my head and sucked in a deep breath, hoping it would give me strength for whatever confrontation lay in wait. Then I plastered on a smile and pushed the door open.

"It's about time. I shouldn't have to call more than once when I need you," my cat chastised despite wearing a giant grin on his furry little face.

"What do you need?" I asked, too exhausted to play nice with him for much longer.

"I know you're under a lot of stress right now, Angela, but I have good news to share. I've asked Grizabella to marry me, and she's agreed." He turned to the newly affianced feline and nuzzled her cheek with his.

"That's great, guys," I said, and I really meant it, too. They couldn't really steal my thunder because no one else could understand their words or the change in their relationship status. "Congratulations."

"Yes, Grizzy and I are thrilled to be spending the rest of our nine lives together. We've been talking and—"

I let out an audible groan and began tapping my foot. *Oops.*

Both cats curled up their faces in disgust.

Grizabella hissed.

Octo-Cat said, "Oh, sorr-ree if our love inconveniences you, Angela. I thought you'd be happy for us."

I sighed again. Really, I was only making matters worse here. Why couldn't I just silently nod and smile until they released me form this room? Me and my big mouth... uh, foot.

"I am. I am. I'm sorry. I'm just stressed about other things," I begged them to understand.

"As are we, which provides a perfect segue to my next point. The two naked creatures can't stay here. This is my house, and now we'll need the space for Grizzy and her human to join us under its roof. I will consent to Up-Chuck's *cohabitery* since he is your mate, but the nude interlopers cannot stay." He lifted his chin as if to indicate the matter was settled.

Yeah, right.

I sighed heavily and wrung my hands. "I've already told you. Where he goes, they go."

"Then I guess he goes too. Sorry, I know you liked him."

I narrowed my eyes in disbelief. "Octavius, you're being very unreasonable and very spoiled."

The Himalayan showstopper gasped. "My sweet, does she always talk to you with such disrespect?"

Octo-Cat clucked his sandpaper tongue. "Far more than I would like, I'm afraid. I really need to train my human better."

The two casts nodded in unspoken agreement.

"Great, well, I'm going," I announced, stomping back toward the door to let myself out.

"I'm not finished with you yet, young lady," Octo-Cat roared after me.

I immediately turned back to glare daggers at my tabby. "You are not my parent." It was getting harder and harder to keep my voice level. In fact, I felt like screaming at the top of my lungs now. I honestly don't know how I managed to restrain myself.

"And a good thing, too, or you would be living in a constant state of punishment. Anyway, if you refuse to meet our very reasonable demand, then we have an alternate offer." The words came out of Octo-Cat's mouth but sounded far more like Griz-abella to me.

"I'm listening," I managed to say without sneering. I hated giving in to this constant bullying, but at the same time, I'd gladly take an easy alternative if it meant getting him to accept the sphynx cats in our home once and for all.

"As you so astutely pointed out, you are *not* our child." He paused to nuzzle his feline fiancée once more. Both their eyes grew wide as they turned back to me. "You are not our child, but we *would* like to start a family. With your help, of course."

Well, this was not what I had expected. I needed

to let him down gently if I could. "Um, this is kind of awkward, but Octo-Cat, you're neut—"

He cut me off with a hiss. "Don't say that terrible word. I know what I am, but Grizabella has done some research, and she tells me that it can be reversible in humans who change their mind about starting a family. I'd like to request that mine be reversed too. Grizzy and I would like to start our family right away. And we'd like to try for biological kittens."

"But, Octo-Cat, you're neut—"

"Bah! Don't say that word!"

Heat rushed to my cheeks. This was not a topic I enjoyed talking about with my cat and his girl-friend. Not one bit. "Your, um, procedure, is not reversible. They cut off your, uh, *hairballs* completely."

"I know what they did," he said stonily, staring off into the distance with unseeing eyes. "But Ethel loved me dearly—that was my first owner, darling —and as such, she must have saved them some-where. Perhaps if you looked in the attic?"

"I..." I began, then, not knowing where to go from there, clamped my jaw shut.

Thank goodness, my phone buzzed with a text. I pulled the tiny screen out of my pocket and read the electronic missive that had just arrived from my mother:

Two minutes away.

A giant, enthusiastic smile bloomed on my face. It was so wide, my cheeks hurt, but I didn't care. I'd been saved from this awkward and un-reproductive conversation, at least for now anyway.

6

stepped out onto the porch to wait for my next batch of wedding guest arrivals. A quick glance around the property revealed that both RVs had been parked somewhere I couldn't see, while the film crew had ventured into the woods that separate my house from the murder house next door. We hadn't gotten a new neighbor since the last one was murdered, and since two former tenants had been murdered within the last two years, I suspected the house was beginning to get the kind of reputation that would keep it vacant for many more to come.

I wasn't sure what the film crew needed in the forest, but I didn't have much time to wonder about it before a black luxury SUV pulled into my driveway and stopped a few feet from the porch. Dad parked while Mom and Grandma Lyn poured out from the back of the vehicle.

"Look who made it safe and sound," Mom crooned as I rushed forward to dole out hugs. At this point I was grateful for all the excuses to wrap my arms around the people I love. So what if I'd given out dozens upon dozens of hugs that day? I still needed more to help soothe my tortured bridezilla soul.

Grandma Lyn only lived a few hours away from Blueberry Bay, but she was uncomfortable driving long distances on her own. As such, Mom had readily volunteered to pick up her long-lost biological mother and make an adventure out of it. And since she never went anywhere without Dad, he got to play chauffeur—a role he seemed to take very seriously, given the suit and dark sunglasses he now wore. From the looks of him, I guessed he was serving double duty as their bodyguard as well. I kept my laugh to myself. My family turned everything into a larger-than-life experience, and I was exactly like each and every one of them. I sure hoped Charles knew what he was getting into.

Just as I finished with the first round of hugs and went in for the second, a red Audi coupe zoomed up the driveway, parking right behind the SUV.

"Mommy, Mommy, we're home!" Paisley cried from the open window of the red car. All eyes zoomed to the little dog, sitting proudly on Sharon's lap in the passenger seat.

Grandma Lyn shot me a questioning glance, which reminded me... "Grandma, could you come inside with me for a quick sec? There's something I need to tell you one-on-one. We'll be right back," I promised my parents as Sharon and Nan continued to fiddle with something inside the sports car without exiting.

I pulled Grandma Lyn into the foyer and shut the door behind us. "There's a film crew here," I revealed breathlessly.

"You hired someone to make a video of your special day? Oh, what a great idea!" my bonus grandma said with joyful tears shining in her eyes.

"No." I dropped my voice to a whisper and pulled her close enough to whisper directly into her ear. "One of the guests brought a reality TV crew here. I didn't know until earlier today. We have to be really careful about, uh..." I paused and glanced around like a crazy person. "About what we can do.

If they catch it on camera, it will not be good for us."

Rather than looking frightened as I was, Grandma Lyn actually had the audacity to laugh. "Oh, Angie. I've been keeping this secret for decades. Believe me, I can be discreet. Was that all you were worried about, or is there something more you wanted to say?"

"That's all," I said, both loving and hating how simple she made the biggest problem of my day seem.

"Then let's get back to the others." She put her hand behind my back and guided me back to the porch where my parents, Nan, Sharon, and Paisley had now congregated.

"What a lovely family you all make," Sharon exclaimed as I realized too late I should have confided in Grandma Lyn about Alpha and his looming threat to ruin the wedding. "Obviously this is your mother," Sharon continued on as she motioned from my mother to Grandma Lyn. "The resemblance is striking. That means the indomitable Nan must belong to you," she said, referencing my father.

Nobody said anything to that, but I watched as Nan's face pinched tight. She knew how much I loved her. Other than Charles, she was the single most important person in my life—and even then, she and my almost-husband were most definitely tied for first place in my heart. Still, she'd had a hard time since Pringle unwittingly uncovered her big secret: that she wasn't biologically related to either me or my mom. We'd only just recently reconnected with Grandma Lyn, and it had been wonderful to welcome her into the family.

Wonderful for everyone except Nan, who couldn't stop apologizing for playing accomplice to her old friend's scheme and for keeping the secret for so long. In all honesty, she never planned to tell us.

But the truth was out there now and we'd been reunited, making our one, big happy family even bigger and—for the most part—even happier.

"Oh, silly me." Nan bopped herself in the forehead, hard enough to leave a subtle red mark behind. "I forgot to stop off at the dry cleaner. I'll just go run out and—"

"No, the dry cleaner is the first place we went after dropping off those two skinny cats," Sharon rather unhelpfully provided. She blew out her cheeks and made a silly face. "Get it, *skinny*? You know, since they're hairless and all!"

Nan completely ignored the poor attempt at a joke as she directed her gaze first to the ground and then to the front door. "Oh, oh, the cats! Yes, I should really go check on them, make sure they're settling in okay."

"Nan," I called out before she could run off. "It's okay. Please don't go."

I thought Sharon understood our unusual family dynamic, seeing as she'd helped me suss out the identity and location of Grandma Lyn, but apparently she had too much in her head to hold on to this one crucial detail. Still, she hadn't meant to hurt anyone's feelings—and she also hadn't meant to upgrade my wedding from a simple circus to a three-ring affair.

I had to remember that.

True friends like Sharon came few and far between; I couldn't say something in anger and risk losing her just because I was feeling a little stressed out.

Grandma Lyn stepped forward and looped her arms around Nan. "We just stopped in to say hello and to see if anyone needed our help," she explained after pulling away.

I met Grandma Lyn's eyes, then quickly glanced sideways toward Sharon, who appeared to be puzzling over what was wrong with what she'd said and didn't notice the unspoken communication happening just in front of her.

"Sharon, was it?" Grandma Lyn piped up. "Why don't you come back with us for a little bit. I'd love to get to know you better."

"Oh, great idea!" I interjected, perhaps a little too enthusiastically.

Our resident reality star beamed. "Sounds perfect as long as I can bring my Chessy. I've already been away for too long, as it is."

"Of course," my mom and grandmother crowed in unison. The words were hardly out of their mouth before Sharon waddled over to the woods and began to call out for her kitty at the top of her lungs.

Well, that explained why the film crew had gone out the way. But why was Chessy canvasing the forest? Could he be in on the seagull's evil plot to destroy my wedding? I definitely needed to devote some more time to doing a bit of reconnaissance, but my day and night were planned down to the minute and I was already running behind schedule as it was.

I wished I could recruit Grandma Lyn to help, but I also couldn't risk hurting Nan's emotions any more than they already were. Plus I was still incred-ibly worried about the film crew, even though she didn't seem to mind at all.

Would I be like that one day, so comfortable with my gifts I no longer feared discovery?

I sure as heck doubted it.

At this point, I could hardly picture my life one day from now—let alone years and years.

Just one more day. I just needed to keep it together for one more day. Then I could reclaim my life for good.

7

Judging by the forlorn look that remained stuck to Nan's face, she and I needed to have a heart-to-heart, but unfortunately there wasn't any time for one. As soon as Mom, Dad, Grandma Lyn, Sharon, and Chessy rolled out, my cousin Mags and her great-aunt Linda rolled in.

"We're here," my fair-skinned, fair-haired, fair-everythinged cousin announced with aplomb.

"Let's get this party started," Aunt Linda trilled. Thankfully, they'd left their kitty overlord Shadow at home. Honestly, while I considered myself a cat person, I couldn't take even one more demanding houseguest without losing my ever-loving mind.

The arrival of my relatives from Georgia meant the last of the out-of-town guests due in today had now arrived. Everyone else would be coming up tomorrow, including a few who planned on flying. I sure hoped no flights got delayed last minute, because we were now less than twenty-four hours from the main event.

Yes, less than twenty-four hours to go.

This was not a drill.

Charles had invited clients, colleagues, and a few local friends along with his family from California, but most of the guest list came from yours truly. The animals I knew had all agreed to watch from the woods, so as not to arouse human suspicion. My friends Bravo and Abigull—the good seagulls—had done a magnificent job tracking down my former clients, witnesses, and accomplices. They'd even invited Gloria, the mama grizzly we'd helped in Katahdin, although I secretly hoped she wouldn't be coming for the sake of all the prey animals in attendance. Although maybe it wouldn't be such a bad idea to call the caterer and ask for an extra ten fish meals just in case.

"Angie, Angie, are you all right?" Mags asked, concern reflecting in her pale eyes. "You kind of disappeared into yourself."

"Sorry, sorry! Just a lot on my mind," I answered truthfully. Apparently Nan and Aunt Linda had already gone inside, because I now stood alone on the porch with my cousin. "How was the drive up?" I asked politely, even as my mind ran away with itself once again.

A dark shadow swooped overhead, and I craned my neck up just in time to see a flash of white feathers disappear over the house. Alpha, that had to be to him!

"It wasn't too bad. We stopped at—"

I hated to interrupt Mags, but I had no choice. "Did you notice any seagulls following you? Or like an otherwise unnatural volume of seagulls?" I demanded, alternating between watching the skies and attempting to make eye contact with my cousin.

Mags worried her lip before asking, "Are you sure you're all right?"

"I'm fine, so long as the seagulls don't ruin my big day—or one very specific seagull in particular." I groaned and shifted my weight from foot to foot. Everything was hurting now. When was the last time I'd gotten a good night's sleep? I simply couldn't remember.

"I guess that explains all the balloons. I saw them peeking out from the backyard as we drove up," Mags said with a grin as she bumped my shoulder. "One question, though. Why do you think a seagull is going to ruin your wedding?"

"Because he said he would," I told her, thinking back to that tense encounter on the pier. "Or at least he strongly implied it."

"We're all done for the day," a man called before stepping out of the forest. Right, the film crew. I had completely forgotten they were here, which meant I'd forgotten to be careful. If I made it through this ordeal—yes, that's how I'd now taken to thinking of my wedding—unscathed in the end, I'd be truly shocked.

"Great, thanks!" I called out to the reality show guys as Mags studied me curiously. Of course, she didn't know a film crew would be here because I hadn't known either.

"We stay too much longer, the lighting will be inconsistent for our shots today and during the ceremony tomorrow, so we're calling it for the day but will be back bright and early tomorrow."

Okay, okay. I didn't need a whole long-winded explanation. I just needed them gone, and they could take the circling seagull with them. I was just about to tell them as much when their front man asked, "Can you recommend a good restaurant where we can grab some grub?"

"Little Dog Diner in Misty Harbor. World's best lobster rolls," I recommended by rote; it had become such an automatic answer to that question I didn't even need to think about it anymore. At least the thought of my favorite lobster roll brought a brief moment joy and relaxation.

"We'll check it out. Thanks, and see you tomorrow!"

And just like that the moment was gone. I sighed as I waited for them to pack up their equipment in the RV they had parked around the side of the house. The fact I failed to notice it proved just how out of it I'd become.

"What can I do to help?" Mags offered. "Put me to work, even if it's just listening."

And that's when it all came pouring out of me in an angry torrent. I told her everything about the complaining sphynxes, the engaged felines who wanted to start a family, about the awkwardness between my two grandmothers, about the minister having to cancel last minute—

"Let me stop you right there," Mags said, placing a hand on each of my shoulders. "I can marry you."

I rolled my eyes at the suggestion. "That's sweet, Mags, but I'm marrying Charles."

She hit me playfully on the shoulder. "Not like that, weirdo. I can marry you both. I can perform the ceremony."

I stared at her, waiting for her to explain how that could even be remotely possible. Thankfully, I didn't have to wait long.

"Earlier this year, around Easter actually, I was doing this TikTok series where I sold blessed candles as part of our new Holy Smokes line. Well, it was a huge hit, and orders were way beyond what Aunt Linda and I expected. It became easier for me to get ordained than to keep visiting the local pastor every time I finished casting another batch. So, yeah, technically I am now a woman of the cloth, you know, in the loosest definition of the word."

"Mags, that's great." Finally one thing had gone right. Was this a sign the tides could be turning in my favor. "You are a life saver. Literally."

"I know," my cousin said with a proud grin. "I make it a point to be awesome. Now what else can I help with?"

"Actually there is one thing," I admitted before leading her inside. I thought I spotted another flash of white moving swiftly across the sky, but it could have been my mind playing tricks on me.

Anything was possible at this point, and that realization terrified me.

"So this little one is Jacques, and the big one is Jillianne. They're Charles's cats, and they live here now, but neither they nor Octo-Cat are very happy about it."

"I don't like how all humans look the same these days," Jacques took a break from licking his paw to say.

"I don't like that she's pawing us off on some stranger," Jillianne wanted me to know.

I worked hard to keep my composure as I explained, "The expression is *pawning off*, not *pawing off*, and this isn't a stranger, it's my cousin Mags."

"I don't like Mags," the larger cat said, then took a swipe at me as if to prove her point.

I shot Jillianne a warning look. Honestly, Jacques probably wouldn't be so bad if he weren't always following her lead. But I also had no way of knowing since it was absolutely impossible to separate them.

"They're from France. Their first owner was murdered, so Charles adopted them a couple years back," I continued to explain to Mags. "And basically they will not stop complaining. I figured maybe you could try to help them get settled in. You know, since you can't hear all the nasty things they're saying, maybe it will be easier."

Mags gasped. "They're saying nasty things? Are they saying nasty things... about me?"

"Noooo," I grimaced as I attempted this little white lie.

Mags caught on immediately. "They are, aren't they?" she grumbled, glancing from naked cat to naked cat. "Well, I guess that's fine. I can't understand them, and I can definitely take them in a fight, so there's that."

"I don't like that you're assigning us a babysitter."

"I don't like that she's talking about fighting us." At this point it didn't even matter which cat was saying what. I was so exasperated with both of them.

"Perfect. You're saving my life once again," I told Mags with an exaggerated smile so she knew how much I appreciated her. "Oh, and while you're watching them, could you maybe also just peek out the window every few minutes and let me know if you spot any seagulls hanging around?"

"I can," Mags said slowly, glancing toward the nearby bay window, "but aren't there good seagulls and neutral seagulls in addition to this one bad one? How will I tell them apart?"

Yikes, she was right. "Okay, scrap the seagull thing then. Just make sure you don't let these two out of your sight."

"You can count on me," she promised with a salute.

That left Alpha to me then.

8

"Are you ready to do the final fitting on your gown?" Nan asked later that afternoon. Things had mostly calmed down now that both guests and vendors were done coming and going.

Mags kept an eye on Charles's cats as promised. She locked both them and herself in one of the spare bedrooms, telling me I was not to come in under any circumstances—otherwise I might spoil her special surprise.

Christine floated around the house offering help here and there, but after I declined her assistance a few times, she stopped offering it. It certainly didn't help that whenever she left the room, our

Chihuahua Paisley ran over to bark at her and herd her back into the room.

"Am I helping, Mommy?" she asked me brightly, wagging her tail so fast it was a blur.

I nodded in response, just to be on the safe side. The film crew was gone, but Octo-Cat's girlfriend's owner didn't know my secret yet, either. She just suspected I was an over-the-top crazy cat lady, which admittedly was also true.

I'd spent most of the last few hours calling guests and vendors to make sure everyone was prepared for their part tomorrow. Thankfully, I was able to place most of those calls while pacing around the yard outside. Unthankfully, I hadn't managed a sure sighting of Alpha in all that time. I'd just need to remain vigilant.

But first, I had a dress to try on.

"I'm ready," I called to Nan, hanging up with the caterer, having just added those extra fish meals as a precaution.

"You look so beautiful in your mother's gown." Nan handed me the carefully hung garment and gave me a little shove toward the stairs so I could get ready. "This time we'll try it with the veil, too, so we can see the full effect," she added with a sweet smile.

As soon as my mother offered to let me alter and wear her dress, I jumped at the opportunity. Nobody was as happily married as my parents—at least not anyone that I knew. That was part of the reason I became so close with Nan growing up. Mom and Dad were always an item, so wrapped up in each other. That left me and Nan as a de facto couple ourselves. She and I have been best friends as long as I can remember, and that was never going to change even after I became a Mrs.

And I could use this final fitting to tell her precisely that. After the awkward exchange with Sharon on the porch, I knew she needed it. That's probably why I rushed when putting on my dress, not even bothering to look at myself in the mirror before bustling back down the stairs.

"I've been thinking," I began, "and I just want you to know that—"

"Oh, Angie! Oh, dear!" Nan exclaimed, bringing both hands to her face, which was growing pale with horror. "What happened to your dress?"

My eyes searched hers for answers. Was this some kind of joke? Because it wasn't very nice, and it wasn't at all like my sweet nan. Perhaps the stress of the day was getting to her as well? I pursed my lips, unsure of what to say.

Nan raised a shaking finger and pointed to my ivory silk train. I twisted to see better and found that in addition to the lace trim and delicate beading, an unexpected new embellishment had been added—long, angry claw marks tore at the fabric, ripping clean through in several places.

My mother's dress! My dress! My big day! Noooooo!

This time when the tears started to fall I was not the least bit surprised. As the salty signs of my sadness rolled down my cheeks, Pringle entered from the kitchen, carrying with him a snack-sized bag of Cheetos.

My eyes grew wide as I watched the raccoon lick orange powder from his black fingers. "Pringle!" I shouted. "How could you?"

He gulped. "How could I what? Oh, I found these in the trash. Someone started but didn't finish them. I didn't take anything new, I promise. Did you know there was a reality show crew here earlier? It's like all my prayers have been answered. Now I Just have to get them to realize I'm a star in the making, and—"

"Why are you in my house?" I demanded, stomping my foot like a fighting bull.

He smiled, completely unaware of the rage

bubbling up inside me. "I was invited. You said as long as I was invited, it was okay to come inside."

I turned sharply, and my dress swirled behind me. "Look at it. It's ruined! Why would you do this to me? Why?"

Now he got it, but he seemed more confused than anything. Probably wondering how he was stupid enough to get caught. Surely, he knew what he'd done was wrong. Yet his words suggested otherwise. "Miss Angela, I didn't touch your dress, I swear. I would never—"

"Out!" I cried, stomping toward the door and flinging it open so hard it hit the wall. "Get out now, and don't bother coming to the ceremony or the reception tomorrow. You will not be welcomed!"

The raccoon intruder dropped the snack bag to the floor and hung his head, then proceeded to stumble toward the door on two legs, looking very much like a depressed *Peanuts* character as he went.

As soon as he was out, I slammed the door behind him. Well, I'd been waiting and waiting, and now this was it. This was Alpha's revenge. The worst part was that Pringle hadn't even realized he'd done anything wrong. I don't know what kind of mind control the evil seagull had managed to exert over the raccoon, but his plan had worked perfectly. He'd recruited an inside man—or at least an animal with relatively easy access to the house—and then he'd gotten him to destroy the one part of the wedding that couldn't be salvaged.

Nan came over and wrapped her arms around me, then hugged me while I shook and cried and cursed the day I ever met that trouble-making raccoon.

"I know someone who can fix it," Nan whispered once my sobs began to slow. "It won't be cheap and it won't be fast, but we can still save the dress."

"In time for the ceremony tomorrow?" I asked, blinking up at her.

She pressed her lips together and shook her head, revealing that tears were shining in her eyes as well. "No, honey, but look at the bright side." She placed her hand under my chin and turned me toward her so our eyes met. "You now have the perfect excuse to renew your vows later—perhaps on your one-year anniversary—and you've also got the perfect dress to do it in."

Instead of having the intended effect, however, that made me cry even harder. I still wasn't sure I'd survive the first wedding. Why on earth would I voluntarily submit myself to a second?

"What do I do now?" I sobbed and accepted a tissue from the box Nan now held out before me. "I can't get married in my pajamas."

She shook her head and pushed a loose strand of hair behind my ear. "Charles loves you. Not some dress. Trust me, honey, it won't matter what you wear as long as you show up at the altar."

I smiled. She was trying so hard to put her own issues aside to help me. At the very least, I could stop worrying about Alpha's revenge now. He'd definitely gotten it, all right. That meant I had no more unknowns to contend with, right? That everything would now go according to plan?

"This is *not* unfixable," Nan insisted, grabbing my hand and squeezing it in hers. "As far as I'm concerned you have plenty of options. Let's see, you could borrow a different dress from your mother. I can stay up all night to make the alterations. I don't mind at all. Or we could borrow a dress from the local theater company. They still have some nice gowns from last month's production of *Fiddler*, and you're roughly the same size as Tzeitel, I'd say. Of course, you could wear a dress you already have, or—oh—we could drive down to the city and do some shopping. We have plenty of time. We can—"

"Nan," I interrupted with a soft laugh. Suddenly I knew exactly what to do. It wasn't the original plan, but I loved it all the same. "I love you, and I appreciate you, but we don't need to do any of that."

"We don't?" she asked, tilting her head in question.

"Nope, I have the perfect idea."

9

t took me a couple hours to hunt down my replacement wedding gown that night, which meant I didn't get to bed until late. I'd hoped to spend some time chatting with Mags, but when I rapped softly on her door, only the sounds of her snoring greeted me. Poor thing seemed just as exhausted as I felt.

I stopped by Christine's room to say good night and make sure the cats weren't being too much trouble, but she just shooed me away. "The cats and I are fine. Go get your beauty rest, wifey!"

Before I could turn to leave, however, Octo-Cat wedged himself in the open door. "We still need to finish our talk," he informed me rather ominously.

"No, no, kitty!" I said in a squeaky baby voice

that people tended to use with their pets. "You need to stay in here tonight."

"I will end you," Octo-Cat growled but fell back a few steps, allowing my escape.

"And next time we talk, I won't be so agreeable!" he called after me through the closed door.

Cats. They were so delusional, every single one of them. And now I'd be owned by three—one of whom liked me okay some of the time and two who actively protested my very existence. *Joy.*

After that, I took a quick rinse-off in the shower, imagining all my worries being cleansed from my body and sucked down the drain. I guess I must have inadvertently picked up a meditation technique or two from Nan over the years. Whatever the case, all these visualization tools were definitely helping curtail my anxiety now. Maybe it wouldn't hurt to join her for yoga a couple times a week going forward.

Soon I would probably take any excuse to spend time with my grandmother BFF. As excited as I was for Charles to move in, I would really miss Nan and Paisley. Maybe I could talk to her about setting up a home office for me over at her place so that I'd have an excuse to spend my days with her. Huh, that wasn't such a bad idea. I might actually guilt myself into getting more work done that way too.

With happy visions of days with Nan and nights with Charles playing in my head, I felt surprisingly calm and happy, considering the way much of the day had played out until now. It didn't take long for me to drift off to dreamland, knowing that the next time I opened my eyes it would be on the happiest day of my life.

I awoke to the sound of hushed whispers. The digital clock on my nightstand had just flipped over to midnight, which technically made it my wedding day.

More whispers invaded my consciousness.

I couldn't tell whether they were coming from outside my window or outside my door. When I got up to check, I saw no one. Hmmm, maybe I was hearing the termites in the floorboards. I hadn't been able to speak with insects before, but why wouldn't my strange gift suddenly grow more powerful at the worst possible time and without any explanation at all?

I strained to hear the whispered words but only grabbed bits and pieces of the conversation. "You go… then I'll… and after that… surprise." Soft giggles punctuated that last bit.

Maybe Mags and Nan were conspiring on that surprise my cousin had mentioned. Yeah, that could definitely be what was going on here. After all, why did strange whispers at night have to mean trouble?

I sorely needed to change my mindset. In fact, I would channel my favorite Chihuahua. I would choose optimism and joy over fear and anxiety.

This was my wedding day, after all, and it was going to be perfect…

Or at the very least, survivable.

I woke up to the ringing of my phone, but before I could answer it, the power zapped from the screen. Shoot. I must have forgotten to charge it last night. I plugged it in and then drifted downstairs to see what the rest of the household was up to.

After putting on a pot of coffee, I went outside with Paisley for her good-morning pee. Nan either wasn't awake yet or had already headed off on one last-minute errand or another. She'd left a nice quiche warming in the oven for me, so I poured myself a cup of coffee and dug in.

Wait a second...

I put on a pot of coffee.

I poured myself a cup.

I was cured!

Or at least my anxiety over the wedding was so extreme, I'd forgotten all about my other very rational fear. I'd been zapped unconscious by a coffeemaker roughly two years ago—that's what gave me my ability to talk first to Octo-Cat and then all animals. And I'd been too afraid to touch the demonic brew machine since...

Until now, that is.

Well, thank heavens for small wonders—or in this case, big ones.

I decided to take my accidental self-sufficiency as a sign. God and the universe were on my side today, and now Charles and I could get hitched without any further hitches.

I chuckled with an almost manic joy as I poured myself a second cup of Colombia dark roast, then floated upstairs as if walking on clouds. My phone had gotten enough of a charge now for me to carefully power it back on—and see that I had missed seven calls, all from an unidentified number. Crud.

I didn't have any voicemails waiting for me, and no new texts either. Whatever these calls were about, I hoped they weren't important. Or rather I chose to believe they weren't.

I'd spent all yesterday worrying and waiting for things to go wrong. Today I wasn't going to waste any more energy on it.

Anyway, prep time was officially up for me. I couldn't go out and run random errands to fix things. I was stuck playing hideaway bride until at last that wedding march welcomed me down the aisle.

It felt strange to have nothing to do after spending all week running around like a headless chicken. True, I would have to get myself dressed and made up, but that wouldn't take long, especially not with Nan, Mags, Mom, and Grandma Lyn to help.

Unsure of what else to do with myself, I placed a call to Charles, just wanting to hear his voice. The next time we spoke after this, he would be my husband—*my husband!*

Instead of my intended, however, his mother was the one to pick up the phone. "Good morning, daughter-in-law," she answered chummily. "Did you forget you're not supposed to speak to Charles until it's time to say I do?"

Oops, I hadn't realized they'd be flying in so

early. Charles must have been up in the wee hours to collect them from the airport.

"We don't need luck," I said with a dreamy smile. "We have love."

My future mom-in-law chuckled good-naturedly. "Just a few more hours, love, then he'll be all yours for as long as you want him."

We said goodbye and hung up. Even though I was a little irritated by Charles's mom playing gate-keeper to our communications, I could respect her traditions. And she was right. It wouldn't be long now.

The countdown had shifted from days to mere hours. Just three hours and twenty-six minutes until *I do.*

And as excited as I was for the main event, even I could handle that short of a wait.

10

padded downstairs to see what everyone was up to. Surely, I couldn't be the first one up. That never happened around here.

I didn't find any of our overnight guests milling about the main floor, but I did spot the TV crew floating around the front yard as if one in mind and body. They had their equipment trained on the long-haired white cat while Sharon spoke animatedly from the sidelines. Whether she was trying to encourage her feline or steal attention, I couldn't say for sure. It made me wonder what Chessy thought of all the constant fanfare. I hadn't had the opportunity to ask him and doubted I would find it. If Octo-Cat were the star of his own show, he'd probably love the adulation but hate the intrusion on his schedule. No, if we were to one day share our exploits with the world, he'd probably prefer a different medium.

Maybe a book series.

I smiled to myself as I headed to the kitchen to pour yet another cup of coffee. I'd need all my strength and energy today, no matter where it came from.

"Oh, good. There you are!" Nan shouted, rushing into the kitchen as if I'd been the one in hiding.

"Here I am," I agreed.

"Well, what are you waiting for? Let's get you gussied up." She took the mug from my hands, set it on the counter, and then yanked me toward the main stairway. We went to Nan's bedroom where a host of cosmetic and hair styling supplies had been set up at her old-fashioned vanity. Grandma Lyn stood waiting by the large picturesque window where Nan typically worked on her various arts and crafts.

"We're going to tag team this one. Right, Marilyn?" Nan said, pulling out the chair in front of the vanity and motioning for me to sit.

Grandma Lyn came over and set a hand on my

shoulder, watching our reflection in the oversized mirror. "That's right, Dorothy."

It made sense that they'd call each other by their first names, but it still felt weird to hear them speak so formally, yet so chummily at the same time.

"I've got the hair," Nan said, grabbing a curling iron and clicking it like a hungry crocodile.

"And I'll do your makeup," Grandma Lyn supplied without taking up any props to prove her point.

This was a good arrangement. I'd been worried that my former Broadway actress nan would attempt to put me in full stage makeup or use the hot pink lipstick she tended to prefer these days. Grandma Lyn's style was much more understated. It had to be, since she'd been hiding a huge part of who she was for decades.

"Where's your dress?" Grandma Lyn asked as she studied the array of cosmetics laid out on the vanity. "Dorothy told me what happened on our drive over. Such a shame."

I nodded and stretched my neck to either side, enjoying the last few precious minutes of free mobility before I was twisted and prodded and warned to keep still. "I'll put it on after we're done. I want it to be a surprise."

"Don't we get a sneak peek?" she asked with a teasing smile.

"Nope. You'll have to wait along with everyone else." I shook my head, drawing an annoyed tsk from Nan who had just started dragging a brush through my sandy locks.

"I still can't believe the raccoon would do such a thing. I thought you said he was turning over a new leaf?" Nan added with a frown.

"Um." I paused and glanced around the room. "Hey, Grandma Lyn, can you close that window?" I nodded toward it, upsetting Nan's progress on my hair once more. Still, I had to make sure there was no way this conversation could be inadvertently recorded for the reality show finale.

My grandma crossed the room and pushed the window shut, locking it for good measure. "I do always love hearing about the local animal drama. So many similarities, but also so much regional flavor." Her eyes glinted as she returned to us at the vanity.

"Well, Pringle—that's the raccoon that lives out back—he's always been pretty nosy. That's how we found out about..." I was about to say that's how we found out about her, my long-lost biological grandmother, but I didn't want to upset Nan. "Never mind."

I moved on quickly, hoping my faux pas went unnoticed. "He's started watching the local AA meetings through the church window and is going through the twelve-step program."

"That's a good thing, right? If only all raccoons attended such meetings, the world would be a much less chaotic place. When I started renting my last house, I chose a neighborhood far from the woods, hoping it would mean fewer masked gossip-mongers, but no such luck."

"Right." I glanced at Nan in the mirror. She appeared to be following along just fine as she began to part and pin my hair. "Well, it would be a good thing, if he hadn't been directed to join by Alpha. He's a seagull I've kind of made an enemy of. And he threatened to ruin the wedding just days before *helping*"—I made air quotes here—"Pringle get his behavior under control."

Grandma Lyn's eyes grew wide as she took it all in. "Oh, so you think the bird is not-so-secretly controlling the critter."

"Bingo." I made a finger gun and pointed to her in the mirror.

"Poor raccoon. Doesn't know enough to know

he doesn't know much of anything," Grandma Lyn said with a sigh.

Nan remained contemplative as she worked my tresses. "I just don't know, sweetie. While I can't speak to the animals personally, I feel like I know them well. And Pringle has a vivid imagination, sure, but he'd never intentionally hurt you in that way. He knows what a big day this is for you."

I shrugged. "I don't know what's going on, but we're past it now. You sent Mom's dress to your seamstress friend already, right?"

Nan nodded while Grandma Lyn rifled through the cosmetics and selected a bottle of creamy foundation and a foam beauty blender to get her work started.

I smiled, choosing once again to focus on the positive, lest I allow the anxiety to consume me as it had for much of yesterday. "So it might not all be going to plan, but it is all going well. I'll be fine. The wedding will be fine. At least I don't have to worry about anything else going wrong now that Alpha's gotten his revenge, right?"

I glanced in the mirror expecting to see twin nods of approval, but instead Nan's face blanched right before my eyes.

"You're mostly right, dear, but there is just one last little thing you should know," she mumbled.

Uh-oh. I took a deep breath and braced myself for the bad news I knew I was about to receive.

"Both the rings for you and Charles... Well, they've gone missing, it seems. But we'll find them! I've recruited Christine to help since your cousin is still working on that surprise for you. But if we don't find them in time for the ceremony, I have other rings you can borrow, your grandfather's and mine, actually. So see? It will still be special. And you can use your own rings when you do your renewals wearing your mother's dress, and—"

"Nan," I interrupted, otherwise she may have continued rambling straight up until it was time for me to walk the aisle. My heart dropped, but I quickly picked it back up off the floor. "The rings probably went missing last night, but we didn't notice because of the dress drama. But it's okay. I'd love to borrow your rings. Thank you for offering them."

She studied me for a moment. "Are you sure?"

"Super sure," I said with an enthusiastic grin. "But maybe we could listen to one of your guided meditation tapes while we finish getting ready?"

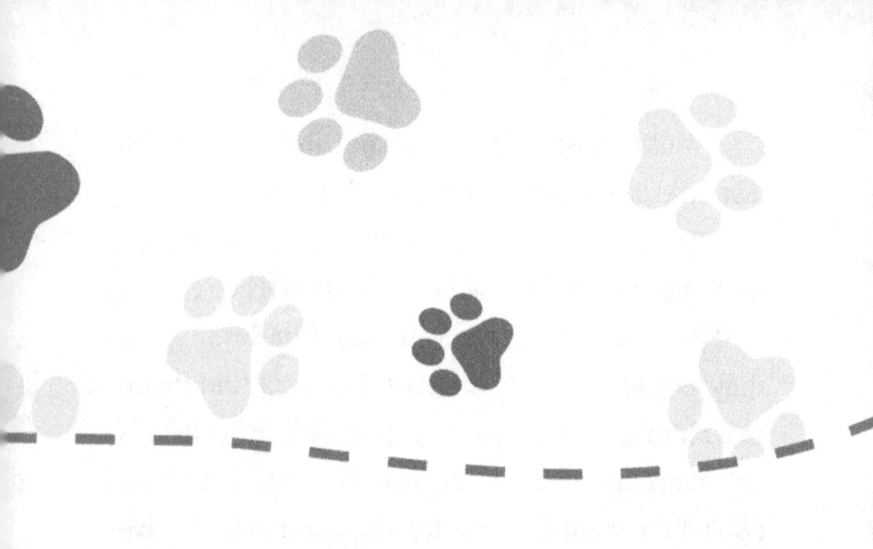

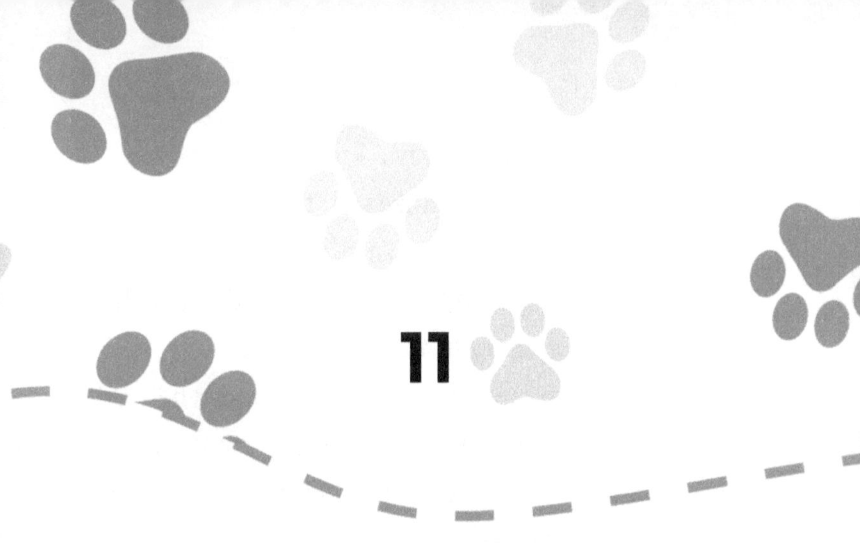

11

blinked at myself in the mirror that hung over Nan's antique vanity.

"Well, Angie. Do you like it?" Grandma Lyn asked with bated breath.

Nan held a hand mirror up so I could see my formal updo from all sides. She'd really outdone herself with this one. Soft curls had been worked into a stylish bouffant with sprigs of baby's breath forming a crown around the edges.

"You two could go into business together," I said with a huge grin as I blinked slowly to admire the deftly applied eye shadow. "I don't think I've ever felt so glamorous in my entire life."

Both women clasped their hands together and cooed happily—showing they were more alike than different, just as I'd always known. Maybe they were finally starting to realize that too.

"Now if you'll just let me fit your veil into place..." Nan jogged over to her bed and lifted the delicate lace accessory from the mattress.

"Your groom is going to lose his mind when he sees you walking toward him down that aisle," Grandma Lyn assured me before both women got to work securing the veil beneath my bouffant.

My heart thrummed with anticipatory bliss. I couldn't wait for the main event, but in the meantime, this moment was its own kind of perfect too. Ever since Grandma Lyn had entered our lives, I'd desperately hoped my two grandmothers could put their divisive past behind them so we could move toward a unified future.

I was just about to say something extremely profound to mark the moment—I'm sure of it—but then my phone rang on the vanity, splintering that picture-perfect moment.

"Oh, could one of you get that?" I begged, realizing I was stuck in place until the veil had been fully secured. "I have half a dozen missed calls from earlier. That's probably them."

Grandma Lyn fumbled for the phone as Nan

continued to work with the veil. She put it on speaker, and I said, "Hello?"

"Hey, Angie. It's Dana. We're in route to your place now, but I realized that my assistant forgot that vegan meal you requested in the warmer. If we turn around, I'm not sure we'll have time to complete our full set-up prior to the ceremony, which means everyone would have to wait before we could start the reception luncheon. I'm so sorry about this, but I wanted to call and check in with you before deciding what to do."

Oof, I wasn't sure what to do, but luckily Nan rescued me from having to decide.

"It's fine. I'll go pick something up," she offered with a grunt, a line of bobby pins stuck between her lips.

"Nan? Are you sure?" I pleaded with her through the mirror, not sure what answer I wanted. I did know one thing for sure though. "I don't want you to miss the ceremony."

"We still have plenty of time. Got a friend in the restaurant biz who owes me a favor. Besides, it'll give me a chance to check in on Grant. I haven't heard from him all day, even though he should've arrived at least an hour ago."

"I'll go with you," Grandma Lyn insisted as she

plucked the various containers of makeup from the vanity and tucked them away in a nylon carrying bag. "Chores are more fun with company along for the ride."

"Okay," I said with a resigned sigh. "Thanks for the heads up, Dana. We've got it covered."

I only knew one vegan, but he was adamant and one hundred percent committed to his lifestyle choice. I didn't want to leave him out while everyone else got to enjoy their meals. Frank from the pet store was a newer friend and not one I wanted to make feel unwelcome, seeing how socially awkward he was most of the time. I considered it a huge compliment that the die-hard introvert was willing to face his social anxiety to celebrate my nuptials.

We hung up and Nan finished with the veil, then raised both arms over her head and let out a little victory shout. "Success!"

I stood carefully and hugged each of my helpers before shoving them toward the door. "Thank you. I love you both. Now get out of here. We have less than an hour until go time, and I need to make sure you're both back and ready for the ceremony."

"Okay, if you need anything—"

"If I need anything, I'll ask someone else. Now shoo!"

The two elderly women rushed out, and one tiny dog rushed in. "Mommy, I'm here!" Paisley shouted by way of greeting. "Oh my gosh, you look so beautiful! Like a Cocker Spaniel or—" Her eyes grew wide with wonderment. "Or a Poodle even!"

I laughed. "Thank you, Paisley. I feel beautiful," I admitted. "Think Charles will like it?"

"He will love it! Although I think you look just as beautiful when you first wake up in your pajamas and your breath smells funny." Her tail wagged so hard, her whole body shook, meaning this was an earnest compliment and not a jab at my unpleasant morning breath.

I carefully knelt down to place a pat on her head.

Paisley shivered and shook happily, continuing to wag that tiny, mostly black body of hers.

I picked the happy dog up and stood again, moving toward the window. "What's going on out there? Anything I should know about?"

"There are men with cameras and big sticks, and a lot of people have started arriving. I've made sure to bark at them all for you."

I chuckled. "Thank you for keeping watch."

She stopped wagging her tail for a moment to say, "It is my sworn duty as your guard dog."

"Of course. What else is going on? Is Charles here?"

Her tail started up again. "I smell him here, but I haven't seen him yet."

We both fell quiet as we surveyed the yard from our secret spot in the window. I couldn't see much with the balloon canopy taking up so much of the area, but I could occasionally make out the silhouettes of people passing beneath.

Paisley's fur bristled and her body stiffened, then she let out a sharp, high-pitched bark. The kind she made whenever she saw another dog anywhere near our yard.

I took it to mean Nan's friend Gertie had arrived with her husky mix, Cujo. Yes, I had a lot of cats in my life, but relatively few dogs by comparison. The energetic Cujo was Nan's running buddy. He'd also helped me with a past case involving the former mayor and his kidnapped golden retriever. Ahhh, memories.

"Shh, shhh," I told the Chihuahua in my arms, stroking her back as I spoke. "They were invited, remember? I promise that no one is coming who shouldn't."

Paisley's ears drooped. "If you're sure."

"I am," I said, even though I wasn't. But who would want to crash a small-town Maine wedding in the middle of the afternoon?

Paisley fixed her eyes somewhere in the distance and spoke with a soft, even voice. "Will you still be my Mommy even after I have to move away?"

Ouch, right in the feels.

"Of course, Paisley. I will always love you, and I will always be in your life. But you know Nan is your human, right? She's the one who adopted you from the shelter, and she'd be very upset if she had to live apart from you."

"But aren't you upset that I'm moving away? I am. I don't want to leave." These words were whimpered. If I wasn't careful, I'd start crying too and ruin the makeup Grandma Lyn had worked so hard to set into place.

"I will miss you lots, but I'll be by almost every day. It won't change that much."

"Do you promise?" She stared up at me with large black eyes shimmering with tears, just as they always did, no matter how she seemed to be feeling.

"I—" Before I could say anything, a loud crash sounded from the hall, drawing our attention toward the door.

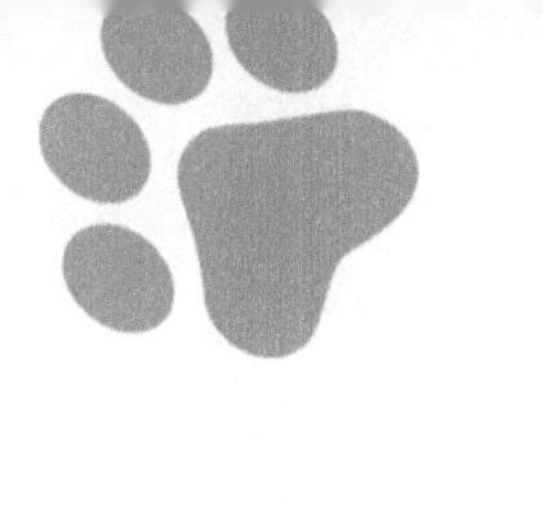

12

"**D**o you think anyone heard us?" a voice whispered from the hall. It was the same one I'd heard last night, but who's was it?

"Probably not, but we should be careful just in case," a second speaker chimed in.

"Then we're ready for the next phase of the plan?" Was this a third speaker? It was hard to tell with how muffled the voices were coming through that door.

"Yes, I think so," one of them said, and then nothing.

"Hello?" I called out when the whispering subsided, but the speakers must have already left.

"Could you tell who that was out there?" I asked Paisley before setting her gently on the floor.

"No, I didn't recognize those voices at all," she yipped in apparent irritation with herself for not knowing. Sometimes she took her duty as watchdog far too seriously, especially since no one was ever afraid of the five-pound shivering fur baby.

"Well, let's go see what all that fuss was about." I strode to the door and pulled on the knob, but it wouldn't budge. What the heck?

This was an old house with many updates and additions made over the years. Because of one such update, the door to Nan's bedroom swung outward while most of the others swung in. I twisted the knob and pushed at the door, but nothing happened.

Okay, this was bad.

Paisley caught on to our current predicament and began barking, "Hey, everyone. We're stuck! Help!"

I traced the room back toward the vanity and picked up my phone, but it was dead again. Okay, I definitely needed to upgrade to a newer model. This thing was not holding its charge at all lately.

Without a working phone, we were well and truly stuck. But surely someone would notice the bride was missing, right? Someone had to be coming to rescue me and Paisley.

"I don't get it," I told her after uselessly attempting the door again. "The knob won't turn at all. It's like we're..."

A horrible realization hit me square in the gut. "Like we're locked in."

Nan had fished out the old skeleton key to her room and locked up last night after the disaster with the dress. "We can't let the same thing happen to your gorgeous veil," she'd reasoned, and I appreciated her so much for it.

She must have left the key in the doorknob, but who would have locked me in? And why the crash?

"Mags?" I called out hopefully. Perhaps she was still in her room working on the surprise she had for me. "Mags!" I shouted louder.

Well, if she was there, she definitely couldn't hear me. She probably had music on her headphones as she liked to do when she worked.

"Christine?" I tried. "Christine!"

This time I received an answer, though it wasn't from the person I was calling.

"What are you shouting about in there?"

"Octo-Cat!" I cried with relief. "Someone locked us in. Can you get help?"

"Just how is he supposed to do that, dear sweet child?" Grizabella interjected. "The only other person who understands us is currently unavailable. We just saw her drive away with the other old woman."

"I've got it covered, my lovely fluffiness," Octo-Cat said confidently. "Be back with help soon!"

I briefly wondered what my cat had planned, but it wasn't long before a giant commotion sounded outside. I cracked the window open so I could better make out what was going on beneath the guise of the helium canopy.

"Eat my hairballs!" Octo-Cat shouted and then laughed maniacally.

Another cat meowed angrily, then hissed.

"Why aren't you talking? Cat got your tongue?" Octavius teased.

Another low growl followed by a sharp hiss.

"You TV stars are all alike. Beauty without brains." Now Octo-Cat hissed, and soon the enraged utterances of two warring felines filled the air.

"This is gold! Are you getting this?" one of the members of the film crew shouted as the chaos shifted from the backyard to the front.

The front door noisily flew open, then several

pairs of feet stomped up the stairs. This was my chance.

"Help! Help! I'm trapped!"

"You, zoom in on the door. You, follow the cats."

"Could you just unlock me?"

"Do you have the shot?"

Whoever he was talking to must have nodded, because at last the door unlocked and swung open.

"Are you okay? What happened?" the lead TV wrangler intoned dramatically, giving me no doubt that this crazed moment would be included in the final cut of their season finale.

"Someone locked me in," I explained, grabbing the key from the lock, then shutting the door between myself and the crew. "Thanks for the help!"

I could still hear them chattering out in the hall. "The bride locked in? Clearly someone doesn't want this wedding to happen. This is even better than I could have dreamed. You got all of that, right?"

The voices receded, and I slumped down to the bed to grab a moment's rest from all the excitement. Paisley must have run out in the commotion because I now found myself completely alone.

Still, leave it to Octo-Cat. His plan had been genius. He must have known the film crew would be unable to resist a good cat fight, and so he picked one with Chessy and then brought everyone up here.

"Hey, let me back in," Octo-Cat called from outside the room, his voice sounding strange. Oh no, I hope he wasn't hurt in all that. I didn't even think about the possibility that Chessy might be able to best him.

I pushed myself off the bed, already missing its comfort, then opened the door just enough to admit the two waiting felines.

Grizabella immediately took up the spot I'd just vacated while Octo-Cat stopped right in front of me and spit something onto the floor at my feet.

Not something. Two somethings.

The missing rings!

I bent down and scooped them up, ensuring they were no worse for the wear. "Octo-Cat, thank you! Where did you find them?"

"Don't worry about it," he said with a satisfied smirk. "I've got your back. Nobody messes with my human's special day."

I didn't point out how taxing his behavior had been just yesterday. Yesterday wasn't the big day, and now today was. I loved knowing he was on my side against any further drama. And even though I still didn't know who had locked me inside the room, I decided that it didn't really matter in that moment.

I could focus on my wedding, or I could focus on this random mystery. And I chose to be truly present so I could remember everything about this day for years to come.

"Nice rings by the way," Octo-Cat said slyly. "Grizabella and I will need something like that to mark our union as well. It's time I made an honest cat out of her."

I sat down on the bed beside Grizabella, and Octo-Cat jumped up too.

I stroked both of their purring bodies and smiled. "I'll be sure to order you both gorgeous bejeweled wedding collars straight away. I'll even let you help pick them out."

The purring intensified, telling me I had gotten my answer just right.

13

Nan and Grandma Lyn returned with the vegan meal twenty minutes before the ceremony was scheduled to begin. They said a quick hello through the door, then excused themselves to finish getting ready. Thankfully, Nan had had the foresight to bring her outfit to one of the guest rooms so she could dress in private—seeing as how we'd co-opted her bedroom as command central for use of its vanity and so I could avoid the second set of stairs that led to my tower bedroom.

With only a short bit of time left to prepare, I put the finishing touches on my gown while Christine and Mags got the cats ready. This included bathing the two sphynx cats, whose tortured howls of protest filled the whole house.

And before I knew it, a soft knock sounded on the door followed by my father's voice. "Are you ready in there?"

I opened the door to my parents' joint expression of love. They were walking me down the aisle together, just like they did everything else that mattered to them.

"I know it's not my dress," Mom said softly, "But this is just as good. You look incredible."

I handed her the decorative bundle I'd put together last night. "Can you hold onto this for me?" I asked. "Make sure no one sees it though."

She accepted my last-minute arts and crafts project, and Dad offered me the crook of his arm. "Well, let's get this show on the road, kiddo."

My replacement dress didn't have a long train, so it was fairly easy for me to get myself down the grand staircase. Still, both parents fussed over me like I was made entirely of glass. Together we reached the main entrance. I could already hear the music playing softly, waiting to usher me down the petal-strewn aisle.

I hiked my dress up a little to protect it from the freshly mowed lawn, then stepped into the yard.

Holding Mom's arm on one side and Dad's on the other, I made my way around the house, then gasped as the backyard came into view.

One hundred white wooden chairs stood in rows, flanking a long aisle. The sunlight streamed through the balloons, creating splotches of color that made the setting look otherworldly, and there, at the very end of the aisle, stood Charles Longfellow, III.

The love of my life, my future, *my husband.*

Tears began to prick at my eyes, but I didn't even care. As the cellist continued her beautiful song, I stepped forward, my parents at my side, all the most important people surrounding me to bear witness to this beautiful memory in the making.

Each step forward was a choice. I was choosing Charles, choosing our love, choosing to leave my old single life to create something new with my partner and best friend beside me for all future steps I would take.

All eyes were on me.

I briefly glanced to either side of the aisle, wanting to remember all the details for later, but it was hard to tear my eyes away from my devastatingly handsome groom. His dark, wavy hair fell in that same perfect swoop it always had, and his bright green eyes sparkled with mirth as he watched me watch him.

Mags stood beside Charles wearing a hot-pink pants suit that she must have borrowed from Nan. She looked incredible and matched the wedding colors perfectly. Nan and Grandma Lyn stood wearing light pink lace bridesmaid dresses, their walks down the aisle already complete. Grizabella's owner Christine was there too, dressed in delicate lace and wrangling the rest of our wedding party—Charles's and my four favorite cats. The boys, Octo-Cat and Jacques, wore hot pink bowties, and the girls, Grizabella and Jillianne, wore delicate pink dresses that coordinated beautifully with the other bridesmaid gowns. The female sphynx seemed quite irritated by the fabric against her skin—she kept nipping at it with her teeth—but Grizabella sat with great poise and obvious pride. The former show cat was no stranger to showing off her beauty for all to admire.

I felt a bit like a show cat myself as the audience oohed and ahhed and murmured soft words of encouragement and approval behind me.

I reached the aisle and took Charles's waiting hands. Mags began to speak, but I didn't hear any of it. My sudden inability to pay attention made me glad the TV crew was here, after all. I could watch my big day on repeat and observe all the tiny details later. Right now, I simply wanted to bask in the moment, in finally having arrived at this place with my very own Prince Charming.

Yup, I'd had a crush on Charles from the moment I first saw him, which happened to be when he stopped by the law firm where I once worked as a paralegal to interview for a recently vacated associate position. We started getting to know each other when he caught me FaceTiming with Octo-Cat at work, and he subsequently black-mailed me into helping with a case where a trauma-tized Yorkie was the only witness to a double homicide.

Speaking of, I'd already spotted both Yo-Yo the Yorkie and her human Mitch in the audience today. I was so glad they could make it, since they'd unwit-tingly played a huge role in the start of our story.

It wasn't until Octo-Cat was kidnapped by his previous owner's disinherited relatives that our tale turned to love. Charles helped me get my missing cat home safe and sound, and then we'd celebrated that victory with our first kiss. The rest, as they say, is history. It's been a wild ride, but one I wouldn't dream of sharing with anyone else.

"Angela Russo!" Reverend Mags shouted, startling me from my daydream stroll down memory lane. "Are you listening to a word I'm saying?"

"Oops. Could you repeat that last bit?" Heat rushed to my cheeks while the audience laughed good-naturedly.

Charles chuckled too and mouthed, "I love you."

"I love you," I whispered back, forgetting to listen to Mags once again.

She waved a hand in front of my face. "Hello? Angie? Do you have vows or not?"

"Uh..." I had, in fact, prepared very personal, very heartfelt vows. They'd undergone at least nine drafts until I was sure they were perfect, but they also seemed wholly inadequate now that the moment was actually here. On top of that, there was an even bigger issue—I was having a hard time remembering them despite how hard I'd practiced.

"Uh?" Maggie prompted as she rolled her eyes, eliciting more bemused laughter from the audience.

"I just want to hurry up and make this man my husband," I admitted breathily. "Can we skip forward to the next part?"

The way my guests laughed at that made me

wonder if I'd missed out on my true calling as a stand-up comedian.

Mags looked toward Charles for his okay.

"I do," he said without taking his eyes off me.

I squeezed both of his hands as a thrill rushed through me. "I do, too."

"Well, I don't," rose a voice from behind the object of my affection. I craned my neck but couldn't see who had dared to rain on my beautiful parade.

"Yeah, I don't either," a second voice chimed in.

And suddenly it all clicked.

The whispers in the night...

The voices I'd heard outside the door right before I got locked in...

I hadn't recognized them because they hadn't been speaking in their usual pattern of complaints beginning in "I don't like."

But this whole time it had been Jacques and Jillianne. At some point, the sphynxes had apparently made it their mission to destroy the wedding, and this right here was their very last chance to do just that.

Unfortunately for them, this bridezilla refused to go down without a fight.

14

I smiled nervously and glanced back over my shoulder toward Grandma Lyn. She was the only one other than me who could understand the animals. Everyone else in attendance just let out a collective *aww* at how cute the kitty bridal party was acting now that they had decided to get in on the ceremony for themselves.

It was good that no one else could hear their protests, but it still hurt my heart all the same. It was especially difficult knowing there was nothing I could do without risking revealing my secret for all our guests—along with all the reality TV junkies in America—to see.

"I don't like this house," Jacques mewled, stepping away from his spot at the altar and crossing in front of me. "And I don't want to live here."

"I don't like your cat, and I don't like you!" Jillianne followed her smaller companion as she hissed, finally alerting the onlookers that something might be wrong here.

Christine, our dedicated cat wrangler, reached for the sphynxes, but they dodged all of her attempts at capture.

I shot Grandma Lyn a pleading look. I didn't want her to miss the rest of the ceremony, but she was literally the only person who could maybe talk some sense into these two naked protestors.

She nodded and moved forward, but before she could cross the altar to the other side, Octo-Cat sprang into action.

"How dare you insult me, and how dare you insult my human on her special day!" he shouted, initiating a cat fight for the second time that day. His hair stood up along his spine, and his tail had grown fat and extra fluffy. "I don't like the two of you either, but I love my human and she loves your human, so that's that. Stop acting like spoiled brats, and fall in line," he growled, then swatted each of the hairless cats in the face.

They stared back at him and wagged their ratlike tails furiously. I imagined that if they had fur, it would also be standing on end.

"Make me say it again. I dare you!" Octo-Cat yowled, wagging his tail now too. I didn't think I'd ever seen him so angry before, and I hoped to never see him this angry again.

Paisley ran over wagging her tail, apparently having no idea what was going on but still wanting to be part of it.

Jillianne reared back and turned toward Paisley.

"Touch the dog, and I will end you," Octo-Cat warned, moving himself protectively in front of the Chihuahua.

"Oh, my man is so brave!" Grizabella swooned, then began licking her paw excitedly.

Grandma Lyn made a grab for Jillianne, and this time she caught the rascally creature. At the same time, Christine yanked Jacques into her arms. Both cats meowed their disdain, but neither managed to break free.

Leading up to the wedding, I'd thought the real threats to my happy day would come from a seagull and a raccoon, but the cats in my life were proving that nobody could out-drama a feline. I'd spent lots of time with Jacques and Jillianne during Charles's and my relationship—and especially since our engagement—trying to bond with the hairless duo. It seemed that all my work had been in vain. As hurt as I was now, I would make it my mission to one day win them over. They were important to Charles, so they were important to me, even if my two step-cats seemed to think I was working full-time to ruin their collective life.

Charles squeezed my hands, and Minister Mags cleared her throat, bringing all eyes back to her. "And that, folks, is why they say to never work with animals or children."

A few strained laughs from the guests punctuated her statement.

"Anyway, let me give you a quick recap of what we've done so far. In lieu of sharing their vows, both the bride and groom skipped straight to 'I do.' So this is the part where I ask anyone with objections to speak now or forever hold their peace."

"I object! Me! I do!" Jillianne shouted from Grandma Lyn's arms and was immediately shushed.

"Okay, no human objections?" Mags quipped, having no idea how right she'd just gotten it. "Then I now pronounce—"

"Wait, not yet, I object!" another voice called from the top of the aisle. Everyone turned as one to view the interloper, but this objection I didn't mind. Instead a huge smile broke out on my face.

"Grant! Where have you been?" Nan demanded from behind me as her boyfriend, the local jewelry store owner, paced quickly up the aisle.

"Dorothy Loretta Lee, it was so hard keeping this secret from you," he sang, striding forward as he reached into the breast pocket of his rented tux and took out a small velvet box, which was hot pink, of course.

"Honey, what are you doing?" Nan stepped forward cautiously and met up with Grant partway down the aisle." You can't just object to my grand-daughter's wedding," she scolded.

"I don't object to the wedding happening. I object to it being over before I get my chance to..." He popped open the box to reveal an exquisite ring made of silver, ruby, and amethyst. "To ask whether you'd like to make it a double. Marry me, Dorothy. Right here, and right now."

Everyone watched as Nan lifted her hands to her face and let out a massive sob. Everyone fell silent as they waited to see what would happen next. Somewhere in the crowd, the reality TV guys were probably high-fiving each other over their good luck.

I watched with wide eyes, standing beside Charles, holding his hand as I myself waited for her response. Surely, Nan would say yes any moment now.

"Grant Gable, I am so mad at you," she said instead with a giant scowl. "You're interrupting my granddaughter's big day and stealing her thunder."

"No, no," I cut in quickly, dropping Charles's hand, then pressing a quick kiss to his cheek. "Be right back."

I stepped away from the altar and rushed toward my bewildered grandmother. "This whole thing was my idea," I revealed with a Cheshire grin.

Nan turned toward me with shock plastered across her made-up face. "What?"

"You're my best friend," I told her, as if something so obvious even needed saying at all. "And you know how I've always had a hard time doing anything without you. Well, when Mr. Gable told me he wanted to propose, I suggested he do it today. We already have everyone we love gathered together, right?" I handed her my bouquet and nudged her toward the altar.

"Is that a yes?" her boyfriend called from behind us.

"Yes! Now get up here right now before I

change my mind." Nan's words were grumpy, but she wore the most enormous smile of her life.

"What do you say?" Octo-Cat spoke up from near my feet as the two brides, two grooms, and one ordained minister reshuffled themselves at the altar. "Care to go for a triple?"

I smiled and lifted him into my arms, handing him to Charles so that I could hold Grizabella. It was the best I could do for a yes without speaking directly to them in front of the cameras.

"Okay, I think we're ready to continue now," I told Mags.

"Never a dull moment," she said by way of agreement, then returned her attention to the guide she'd printed out from the Internet. "Okay, folks. You're now getting a two-for-one. Lucky day! Let's take it from the top!"

15

did.

Charles did.

Nan and Grant did.

And of course, Octo-Cat and Grizabella did, too. I'd have to make up a special certificate for those two crazy kittens later, but in the eyes of God and one hundred assorted guests, we were all now officially wed.

"You're my husband," I told Charles, rubbing my nose against his after he'd finished kissing his bride to the delight of all who had gathered.

"You're my wife," he answered with a toothy grin before claiming my mouth a second time.

"I said kiss the bride," Mags teased over the

growing din. "Not have a full-on make-out session with her."

Charles and I broke apart, then kissed again.

And again.

And—you guessed it—*again.*

Everyone laughed. There was so much laughter that day. It's one of the things I liked best about it.

Grandma Lyn tapped me on the shoulder. "I'm just going to take the cats inside while you do your processional," she whispered in my ear.

Right, the processional. Okay.

I could see some of the guests starting to get antsy as they waited for Charles and me to make our ascent up the aisle. I motioned to my mom. "It's time," I called and gave her a quick nod of confirmation.

She jumped up and delivered the bundle I'd entrusted to her. Yesterday, after purchasing my 90s-tastic gown from the Salvation Army, I'd stopped off at the dollar store to stock up on supplies. The end result was a bouquet of multi-colored sharpies, each with a faux flower glued to its cap. The result was clearly homemade but also really quite pretty.

"You'll be first," I told Mom as Charles and I

arranged ourselves beside the first aisle of white wooden chairs.

"First to what?" Mom glanced from me to the markers and back again. "You couldn't possibly mean—"

"I'm a living guestbook," I said, untying the crafty bouquet and fanning out the different colors before her.

"You'll ruin your gown," she warned, meeting my smile with a tense expression.

"Nah, I'll just make it better. This way everyone who was here gets to contribute to this special memento. Besides, it's going to look so cool when it's all signed! Now pick a color, pick a spot, and write on me, Mom." I nudged the markers toward her again, unwilling to flinch on this.

She shook her head and laughed. "You always did march to your own beat, Angie Russo."

"That's Angie Longfellow to you, missy."

We both tittered at this while she selected a place on my torso and wrote in purple marker. When she finished, I asked what it said, unable to make out the script since my sizable chest was in the way.

"That I love you," she said, offering both me and

Charles a quick peck on the cheek. "And I'm so, so proud of you."

We hugged, and then it was Dad's turn. He chose red but wouldn't tell me what he wrote. He said I could find out later after I'd gotten changed into something else. When he moved on, Charles let me know that he'd written the classic Dad threat, telling Charles to treat his little girl right... or else.

Nan and her new husband stood beside us greeting each guest along the processional. Nan and I had many of the same friends to begin with, and I'd also helped Grant sneak in some of his friends without her noticing. Octo-Cat and Grizabella had been escorted back inside by Grandma Lyn and Christine, but I think they preferred it that way.

I glanced toward the woods and spotted a few of my animal friends watching from the protection of the trees. Irving the giant buck who had witnessed my former neighbor's accidental death stood with a family of squirrels sitting on top of his head. It was hard to tell for sure from this distance, but I think one of the squirrels was my old friend and helper Maple. It looked like she too had fallen in love and already had a huge family to prove it. Good for her.

A fluttering of white among the trees drew my

eyes up just as two seagulls took to the skies. That would be Abigull and Bravo, my friends who had promised to watch from the woods. And so they had.

"You've got yourself a good one," Officer Bouchard told Charles as he clapped him on the back, then selected a black marker from my hands and stooped down to write a message near the hem of my dress.

I loved this.

The ceremony had been all about me and Charles, but now with the processional, I was able to focus on each of my guests in turn. I couldn't wait to celebrate with everyone at the reception. I hoped they were all having a great time, like I was.

It seemed that, excepting a few minor bumps along the way, this whole day had been filled with perfect moments from start to finish. And it wasn't even close to over yet!

"I love you," Charles said suddenly, then grabbed me in his arms and tipped me back as if part of a dance. If not for his strong arms, I surely would have fallen. Instead I got another earth-shattering kiss as I clung to my brand-new husband.

"Congratulations," a voice I hadn't heard in a very long time muttered as soon as we came up for air. It took me a moment to regain my senses, but when I did, I recognized the Calhoun twins—Charles's former girlfriend Breanne along with my one-time crush, Brock, who after being arrested for a crime he didn't commit had decided to turn over a new leaf and change his name to "Cal."

"Thanks for coming," I told them both, even though I wasn't super happy that Charles's ex had shown up on our happy day. I probably should have expected this, but it still mabe me wonder: Was she here to try to ruin something? Well, she could get in line behind Jacques and Jillianne as far as I was concerned.

"You make a very handsome groom," Bree said, placing both hands on her hips and drawing attention to her above-the-knee green dress, complete with plunging neckline.

"And we'll just be going," her brother said, yanking at her before she could try to lay a hug on my new husband.

"Thanks for coming," I yelled after them, even though I'd already said that once before.

Charles pulled me to him and pressed his forehead against mine, creating a little bubble just for the two of us. "Sorry about that. I told you not to invite Cal. He always shows up with her as his plus-one," he said.

"It's fine. She's fine," I said with a soft laugh. Charles had already chosen me over Breanne a thousand times over. I wasn't jealous of her desperate ploy for attention. If anything, I felt kind of bad for her. Hopefully she'd find love of her own someday soon.

I'd stopped paying attention to what she was up to after she and Charles broke up. As far as I knew, she was still in the real estate business and doing well.

Last I'd heard, her brother had given up his handyman gig and gone back to school. He wanted to be a lawyer now, imagine that. I guess being wrongly maligned and imprisoned gave him a deep sense of justice, and I admired him for turning his horrible ordeal into something positive for the world.

"Ready for me?" another familiar voice prompted, drawing Charles and me back to the task at hand.

"Bethany!" I shot forward and hugged my former frenemy tight. I hadn't seen Bethany Peters since she moved to Georgia to look after her delinquent cousin Peter, who had thankfully chosen not to attend today's ceremony.

"How have you been?" I gushed, thrilled to bits that she was here now. All that frenemy stuff had been nonsense. I wished I had taken more time to get to know her when she still lived so close. I couldn't change the past, but I could do better going forward.

Another vow for today, and one I intended to keep.

"We'll catch up at the reception," she promised. "Oh, and I brought you a special essential oil blend I made. It's for wedded bliss. Put two to three drops in your diffuser daily, and you'll live happily ever after."

"I will, thank you," I said as she signed my gown in turquoise. She'd always been oddly obsessed with essential oils, and while I'd never been a fan, I would happily take her up on this promise of wedded bliss.

Even though I highly suspected Charles and I would not be needing any help in that arena.

16

And then it was time for the reception. Thankfully we had a huge yard, so we simply had to shift the party over to where twelve circular tables of eight and one long rectangular head table were already set up and waiting. A bonus table sported a host of wrapped packages and a big basket where guests had dropped their congratulatory cards.

Charles had wanted to create a bridal registry, but I insisted it was way more fun not knowing what people might buy. Since I'd won that argument, I had no idea what types of gifts filled the table, but I knew finding out after our honeymoon would be great fun. One of the presents made me a little uneasy though. It was suspiciously wrapped in old junk mail circulars and not very skillfully at that.

"Do you think it could be a bomb?" the boom mic operator asked his buddies as the film men zoomed in on the odd present.

"Oooh, I hope so. That would be awesome!" another of his crew answered. Well, glad to know they were on my side. Entertainment over excellence, I supposed.

My mom had fully taken over MC duties from Mags now that the reception was on. She was quite comfortable in front of a camera thanks to her job as a big-time local news anchor. I assumed the TV show guys didn't know that—and that she didn't want them to—because they spent very little time focusing on her or my dad, the semi-celebrities in our midst.

They had figured out that Mags was something of an Internet celebrity, though, and had foisted their star feline Chessy into her arms as they recorded the both of them.

"Ladies and gentlemen, please welcome Mr. and Mrs. Charles Longfellow, III!" my mom announced in her reporter voice as Charles and I rushed out onto the shiny dance floor that had been laid in the yard for just this purpose.

Charles spun me to the delight of our guests, then pulled me close to his chest as our cellist began to play "My Funny Valentine." We swayed together, heart to heart, as Charles serenaded me with the song he had sworn would always be ours.

The music ended far too soon for my liking, but at least we still had so many more festivities ahead. Our guests cheered and started clinking their wine glasses, indicating that they wanted us to kiss. No problem there!

A second song began to play, and we cleared off the floor to give Nan and Grant space for their first dance as a married couple. While we'd gone with a timeless classic, they'd selected something hugely inappropriate that I recognized from the current radio hits. I think it was a Cardi B song. Either way, I did not want to know how or why this became my eighty-something grandmother's go-to love song. I did not want to know even a little bit.

When the music ended, Nan pulled me and Charles back toward the house. "C'mon, there's a surprise for you inside. We'll be quick, but I wanted you to see."

Back in my giant manor home, nothing was as

I'd left it less than an hour ago. The furniture had been cleared out and a baby gate had been erected at the bottom of the grand staircase.

"Hello and congratulations!" Nan's friends Gertie and Pearl chimed as we went further into the house. Pearl had taken over at the animal shelter after the last director was caught embezzling, and Gertie had become Nan's closest friend thanks to all the visits that followed her early morning runs with Cujo. They stood beside a trio of incredibly tall cat trees that were ringed by several bowls of both dry and wet cat food. Some loose catnip had also been scattered on a large throw rug they'd brought, and I could already see Beans from the pet store rolling around and rubbing himself in the stuff.

"It's a reception for all our animal guests!" Nan announced proudly and with jazz hands. "Didn't want them to miss out on the celebrating."

I heard footsteps on the stairs and turned just in time to see Octo-Cat and Grizabella jump over the baby gate in unison. They walked side by side so close they were touching, then scaled the tallest cat tree and took up post at the very top. The two barely fit up there together, but somehow they made it work.

Nan leaned in to whisper, "I suspected he'd

make your day all about him, so I figured we might as well give him a party too."

I beamed and gave her a wink, letting my grandmother know just how right she was about that. True, she couldn't speak with the animals, but she understood them all the same. I didn't see the sphynxes anywhere, leaving me to wonder whether Grandma Lyn had shut them in a room so they could think about what they'd done. I hadn't known her for long, but that seemed like the kind of thing she might do.

"Thank you for coming to our wedding celebration," Octo-Cat meowed from the top of the tree. "You may leave your gifts at the entrance. And be warned, nobody look at my beautiful bride too long, or I'll cut ya!" He flexed his claws demonstratively, and Grizabella nuzzled him with great gusto. Apparently she liked the tough guy act. To each their own, I guessed.

"I love it, thank you!" I gushed, realizing I hadn't said anything at all. I'd been too busy taking in the spectacle.

"You're very welcome, Angie," Pearl chortled and fluffed her short hair. "I hope you don't mind, but I brought a few adoptable pets too. Maybe you could just make it a point to mention that to the guests? It would be great to find these cats homes. What a way to leave a lasting mark on your big day."

I agreed that of course I would make an announcement. I wanted the homeless pets to find their place too, but if you asked me, our wedding had already left quite a mark.

"We will do just that," Charles answered for the both of us, lacing his fingers between mine, then lifting our joint hands and placing a kiss on the back of mine.

"I wish EB didn't have to miss out," Grant said with a wistful smile as he talked of his gray rescue lop rabbit named EB, short for Easter Bunny, which is precisely what she was before he rescued her. "But she probably wouldn't enjoy hanging out with all these predators."

Nan rubbed his back and laid a head on his shoulder but said nothing.

"As the first order of business, I would like to uninvite all the dogs. Thank you for coming. Good-bye!" Octo-Cat decreed from his prime perch, then added, "Except Paisley. Paisley can stay."

"He's being a real piece of work again. Isn't he?"

Nan whispered in my ear as Charles squeezed my hand knowingly.

I bit back a laugh. Yes, the people in my life definitely understood me, and I wouldn't have it any other way.

17

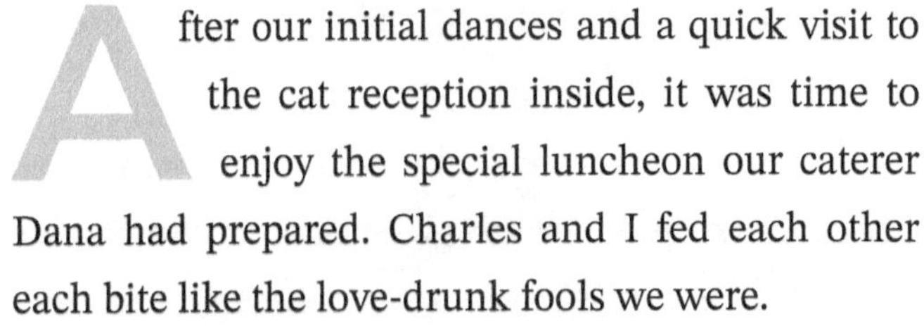

After our initial dances and a quick visit to the cat reception inside, it was time to enjoy the special luncheon our caterer Dana had prepared. Charles and I fed each other each bite like the love-drunk fools we were.

I did pause briefly to make sure Frank was enjoying his vegan meal after all the special measures we had to take to get it for him. He seemed happy enough with what looked like a mixture of beans and rice and fajita veggies. He caught me staring and offered an awkward wave before returning his full attention to the food in front of him.

I eyed the woods to see if my animal friends were still watching from the sidelines, but they appeared to have cleared out and gone back to their daily lives. I'd have to thank them for coming later. It really did mean a lot that they'd shown.

Pringle, for his part, had stayed away as I'd instructed. A part of me felt bad for exiling him, but I just didn't want to risk him ruining anything else—whether intentional or not. Nan believed he had good intentions, and based on the little show with Octo-Cat at the kitty party inside, she did understand the animals in our lives quite well. Still, I didn't know if I could ever really trust the raccoon again.

"Everything okay?" my husband asked after we'd polished off our shared plate of fish.

I kissed him, which one of our guests saw and began clinking her water glass. Soon a chorus rose up asking us to kiss again. Like I needed a reminder to kiss my husband.

"Everything is wonderful," I told him, still leaning in close. "I'm just thinking about Pringle."

A sudden wave of concern flooded Charles's shining green eyes. "I haven't seen him around. Is he okay?"

"Oh, man. You have missed out on so much, thanks to your mother wanting to keep us separated for tradition's sake."

He nuzzled my cheek, much like I'd seen Octo-Cat do with Grizabella. "Thank you for doing that. It meant a lot to her," he whispered, then kissed me again.

I leaned into him with a happy smile. "Of course. There's just so much to catch you up on, and with a certain film crew roving about, I'm not sure I can do it right now."

"Later then," he said with a dopey smile of his own. "We do have the rest of our lives together, after all."

"Ladies and gentlemen. Honored guests."

I glanced up to find Mags standing beside the cellist after having coopted the microphone from my mother. "Just because the bride and groom chose to skip their speeches doesn't mean I won't delight you with mine. Buster, roll tape."

I had no idea who Buster was, but apparently he was listening because right on cue, someone set up a projector screen behind Mags, and a film began to play for all to see. It began with a photo of me and Charles taken at the altar, then splintered into hundreds of tinier pictures that showcased Charles and me both together and apart. The Frank Sinatra version of "My Funny Valentine" played in the background, but even after it stopped, the pictures kept flashing by onscreen.

Now that the music had ended, Mags took over narrating. "Big shout-out to Mama Longfellow who provided the pictures of Charles, and to the many, many folks who shared photos of Angie. This one's my favorite by the way."

Everyone laughed at the photo of me and Mags bundled up against the cold sporting red noses and hot cocoa at the holiday festival downtown where two people had been murdered in an ice sculpture garden—they probably didn't know about the murders that happened shortly after this photo op though.

"Aunt Linda is now coming around with some mementos for everyone," Mags boomed next. "Show them what you got, Aunt Linda!"

Maggie's great-aunt waved and then held up a gorgeous candle made in our wedding colors. The bottom layer was hot pink, the middle layer was an understated softer hue of the color, and the top had been cast in white. The finished candle had then been carved carefully to reveal a big cursive *L* protruding from the rest of the design. *L* for Longfellow. That was my name now. Aw, heck yeah.

"I want one!" I shouted, and Mags rolled her eyes. "Duh, I made a ton extra, and they're all yours. Light one each year for your anniversary and think back to this special day. Love you, cuz!"

She then went on to tell me in great detail just how much she loved me and how much richer her life has been since we found each other. Mom and Dad made speeches too, along with Charles's parents. It all boiled down to how much everyone loved us, thought we were a great couple, and wanted us to live a life of happiness and love.

All the speeches made me tear up, but it was Nan's new husband Grant who really pulled at my heartstrings. He took center stage with his bride, pulling her out onto the dance floor and holding one of her hands in his while hanging onto the microphone with the other. His words were projected for all to hear, but his message was clearly just for her.

"I know we don't have many years left, but I look forward to spending every last one of them... every last day, minute, second, with you. I didn't think there was anything left for me in this life, but then I found you and that all changed. I feel like a young lad again, and I'm the happiest I've ever been. Who knew that our golden years would truly be the best of our lives? I love you to the moon and back, Dorothy Loretta Lee Gable, and I will keep on loving you until this old heart can love no more. Until then, every beat will be shouting your name so that the whole word knows exactly who it belongs to. My wife. My best friend. My whole world."

I swear there wasn't a dry eye in the place after that one.

The cellist began to play again, inviting everyone onto the dance floor.

"I love you like that," Charles told me before offering another kiss.

"I love you like that too," I responded, and kissed him again. One day I would have to share the vows I'd written just for him. Maybe I could recite them on the long drive to our honeymoon destination.

The honeymoon was a gift from my parents. For one week we'd be staying at a stately old home in the heart of Richmond, Virginia. The place boasted an enormous garden made private by a tall brick wall around the perimeter. Somehow my parents had managed to book the entire enormous estate just for the two of us. It would be a bit of a drive, but Charles had insisted on road-tripping it rather than flying. We'd sat down together weeks ago and planned each stop along the way to extend our trip into a truly memorable affair.

We'd leave tomorrow morning since we planned on partying late into the night. Nan and Grant would have free rein of the place until our return. Before Nan had realized that she would be married too, she'd agreed to wait an extra couple weeks before moving out so she could pet sit while Charles and I were away.

Once again I found myself torn between enjoying the moment I currently found myself in and anticipating all the good things that would happen next. First world problems, I tell you.

"Excuse me." Someone poked me in the arm as Charles and I swayed together to another one of Nan and Grant's questionable song choices.

"No cutting in. I'm not ready to let her go," Charles mumbled without even looking at the interloper.

"I don't want to dance," the other man said in a deep, almost threatening voice. "I want to be given what I'm owed, and I'm not leaving until I get it."

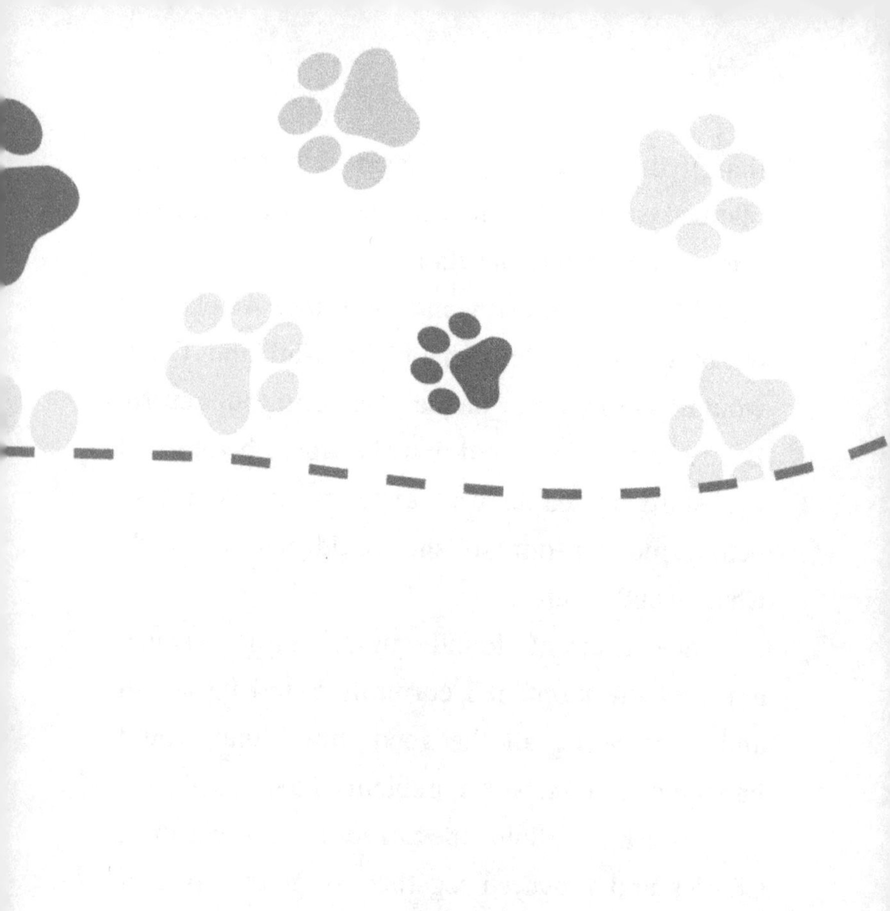

18

stopped dancing and turned toward the man in shock. Charles continued to hold me close, protectively even. It took me a minute to place our unfriendly guest without his wares, but this was undoubtedly the same vendor who had taken several trips out yesterday to set up our massive balloon canopy.

"I'm sorry. What?" I asked, blinking back my surprise. He'd been so amiable yesterday, if also a little put off by my obvious struggle to maintain composure.

"You left me waiting on your porch for almost an hour," he sneered. "I told you I needed to be paid that day, and instead of saying you didn't have the funds, you ghosted me!"

"What? No! I paid you." How dare he show up at my wedding and cast insulting accusations at me like this?

"I don't like how you're talking to my wife," Charles interjected, fixing the balloon vendor with an equally hostile stare. "Either adjust your tone, or leave."

The other man scoffed, refusing to back down. "Well, buddy, your wife didn't pay me, and then she also wouldn't answer my calls."

I gasped as some of the pieces began to click into place. "Were you the unknown number? Why didn't you leave a message?"

"Your voicemail was full. I didn't even get the option. I did a big job for you, and I deserve to be paid for it. Now since you wasted my time by making me take yet another trip out here, I'm afraid I'm going to have to charge you an extra ten percent late fee. And if you don't pay me right now, I'll sue you for all you're worth and get much more."

My lawyer husband bristled at this careless and uneducated threat, but I placed a hand on his chest to indicate that he should hold his tongue.

I thought back through the timeline in my head. I remembered the vendor coming back yesterday and asking for payment. I remembered going upstairs to get the check, and then...

Then I helped Christine with one thing and Octo-Cat with another. I'd called Charles. I'd talked to the reverend who had to cancel. I'd lain on my bed and cried...

But I never actually went back downstairs with that check.

"Gosh, I am so sorry," I cried, and the aggressive vendor's face immediately softened and his words became more kind.

"It's okay," he said. "I could tell you had a lot on your mind, and I know how weddings are. But it's the end of the month, and I need that check from you to make my mortgage. You understand, don't you?"

"What's the bill?" Charles asked with a sigh, pulling out his wallet. He still seemed rather worked up about the vendor's less than affable approach to collecting what he was owed.

The vendor told him what it amounted to, and Charles handed him a wad of cash. "Keep the extra. Sorry for the inconvenience."

"Thank you! Congratulations!" Now that he was paid, Mr. Helium was quick to depart.

"Why do you have all that cash?" I asked my

husband, perplexed by the huge sum he'd had just waiting and ready to go. It saved me from having to run inside to grab my checkbook, but—as the kids were saying these days—was also a bit *sus*.

He shrugged. "Had a client pay yesterday in cash. I was going to take it to the bank, but then thought we could use it on our honeymoon for all the lavish dinners and spa treatments we plan on having."

"I like how you think," I said, relaxing into his embrace as we resumed our dance.

"Mmm" was his only response as he pressed his lips to my forehead. We swayed for a little longer until my cousin's voice rose high above the crowd.

"I already told you. I don't want to do your stupid show!" she practically screamed at the film crew surrounding her.

Sharon, wearing the same gown she had upon arrival yesterday, tried to push into the group and draw attention back to the cat in her arms, but no one paid her any mind.

"You're funny. You're beautiful. And you make honest-to-goodness candles! And fancy videos, too!" one of the reality TV guys insisted. "You could be the biggest thing since *Keeping Up with the Kardashians*!"

"Eww, pass." Mags held up a hand to block her face, but the disgust in her voice made her feelings on the matter clear.

Charles tugged me over to the dramatic scene unfolding across the dance floor. "Excuse me. Is there a problem here? I'm Ms. McAllister's attorney and would be happy to discuss this harassment in a more formal setting."

"We were just going," one of the men groaned, and like magic the unit floated away.

"Sorry about them," Sharon said with a pitiful look on her face. "I thought they were excited about the wedding because of all the cats that would be in it, but it seems like they were just looking for their next big show idea. They were never planning to renew me and Chessy."

I put an arm around her shoulders. "Did they say that?"

She nodded glumly. "This morning, and they've been horrible to me ever since. I have a feeling they're only filming Chessy still so they have enough to wrap up the season and make a good portfolio piece for wooing bigger and better stars."

"I'm sorry. We still think you're a star," I said, and Charles and Mags bobbed their heads in enthusiastic agreement.

"Want me to show you and Chessy how to cast candles?" Mags offered magnanimously. "We can put it on my YouTube channel. I have more than a million subscribers, you know."

Sharon's eyes lit with renewed excitement. "You don't say? One million? That's far more viewers than our little TV show ever had. Yes, please sign us up!"

It seemed once someone got bitten by the fame bug, there was no recovering. The Sharon I originally met pre-show had been so quirky and full of life. Now she just seemed sad and desperate for attention. I hoped that after the excitement from the show died down a bit, she could go back to being her normal fabulous self.

Meanwhile I would do my best to keep out of the limelight, secrets and all.

Something moving low and close to the ground caught my eye. Octo-Cat was creeping around the outdoor party and had just swiped a leftover filet of fish from someone's plate.

"What are you doing out here?" I asked in that singsong voice I used when pretending to be a normal pet owner.

He finished chewing and then gulped the fish

down. "Need you inside," he mumbled, then ran off, expecting me to follow.

I waved to Charles where I'd left him on the dance floor, and he waved back, despite appearing to be deep in conversation with my former boss, Mr. Richard Fulton. He'd been senior partner at the firm before Charles arrived, which meant that this was the first time the two were meeting.

I wondered what they could be talking about. Probably just lawyer stuff.

Well, at least he would be occupied while I checked on whatever it was Octo-Cat needed from me. I knew better than to keep that feline of mine waiting, and I still owed him big for his help finding the lost rings and wrangling the protesting sphynxes during the ceremony.

I'd have expected him to be fully immersed in his new wife Grizabella rather than worrying about the likes of me.

Made me wonder what he wanted now.

I guessed it was time to go find out.

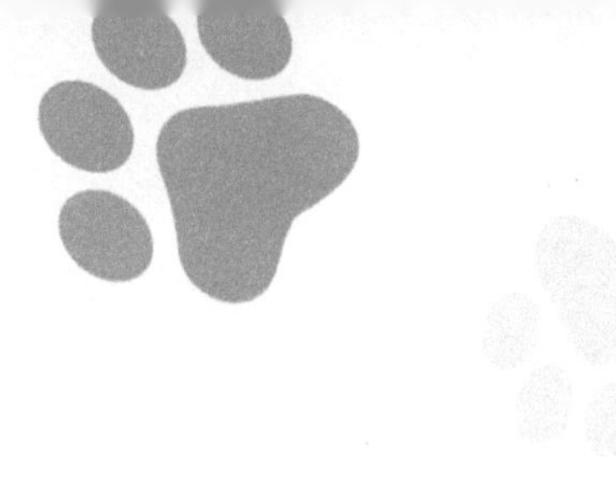

19

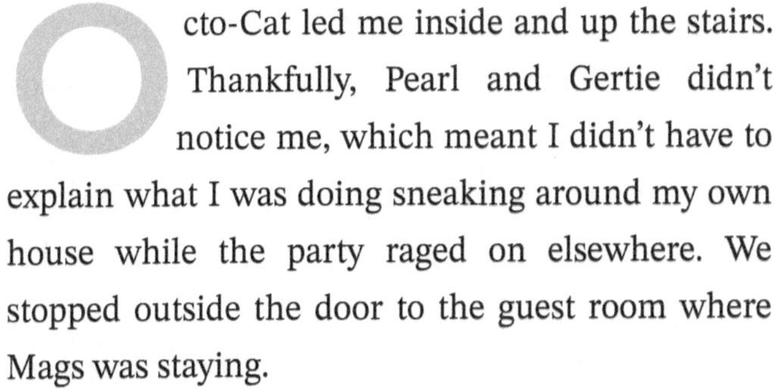

cto-Cat led me inside and up the stairs. Thankfully, Pearl and Gertie didn't notice me, which meant I didn't have to explain what I was doing sneaking around my own house while the party raged on elsewhere. We stopped outside the door to the guest room where Mags was staying.

"We did all our talking through the door, but you can go ahead and open it," my cat informed me.

I carefully let the both of us inside and found Jacques and Jillianne curled up together on the bed to share warmth.

"What's going on?" I asked, glancing from my tabby to my husband's hairless felines.

Jacques stood and stretched forward, revealing

the webbing between his toes. No matter how many times I'd seen the way he moved, I couldn't help but be transfixed. The most horrifying thought? That all cats looked this way under their fur, even my Octavius.

Octo-Cat hopped up on the bed, and I sat down too.

"Well, go on with it already. Just like we discussed!" he growled impatiently.

"I don't like that I hurt your feelings," the black-and-white skin-cat said.

"Not like that," Octo-Cat corrected with a flick of his tail. "Speak like a normal cat, or don't speak at all."

Jillianne growled in defense of her little brother, but Octo-Cat quickly shut her down with another stern glance.

"I'm sorry," Jacques mewled pitifully. "We were bad kitties."

Jillianne remained pointedly quiet, so I kept my focus on Jacques. Now that he was being nice to me, he was kind of cute, actually. All those wrinkles were endearing, and the fact that he had a light fuzz on his feet and ears but zero fur on the rest of him was also charming.

"It's hard for us to be back here after the

senator died. We still feel guilty about what happened, and we really miss her," little J continued.

Yes, their former owner had been the first corpse to turn up next door. After Octo-Cat and I solved the case, Charles had agreed to give the two pedigreed cats a new home with him so they wouldn't need to spend any time in the rescue or risk going to separate families.

"Why do you hate me?" I asked, never understanding what I'd done wrong when I was the one who had proven their innocence and had worked so hard to bond with them since.

Jacques shook his head. "We don't hate you, but we don't want things to change. It was hard after the senator died, but eventually we started to feel happy again with Charles. Now everything's changing. New family. New house. We're scared."

"You don't have to be scared. And you can always tell me how you feel. I want you to be happy here. And I want to help however I can."

"Told you," Octo-Cat sang with a satisfied smirk. "She may be just a human, but she's the best one there is."

I puffed up with pride at that. I would never stop being shocked and delighted by my cat's somewhat rare shows of affection. He was really spoiling me today, too.

I reached a hand toward Jacques, and he stretched into my palm, letting out a rumbling purr. He felt like a warm peach, not entirely unpleasant but definitely not anywhere near normal.

Octo-Cat crossed the bed and nudged Jillianne with his paw. "Now you."

"He already said it. Why do I have to?" she groused.

Octo-Cat swatted her again, this time with claws.

"Fine," she snarled, then rose to her feet. "I'm sorry. Everything Jacques said is true, okay?"

"And what else?" my cat prompted with another flick of his tail.

Jillianne sighed and mumbled something I couldn't quite make out.

Octo-Cat grabbed her by the skin of her neck and flipped her over while still holding on with his teeth and all four of his legs. "We can do this the easy way or we can do this the hard way," he mumbled, his mouth full of kitty flesh. "It seems you've chosen the hard way."

The black lady sphynx breathed heavily, her eyes wide.

"Just do it, Jilly," Jacques said softly. "We already tried being bad, but it didn't work. Let's be good now. Pretty please." Even though I knew Jacques was three years old, he sounded like a baby then as he pleaded with his older and much crankier sibling.

"Fine," Jillianne spat. "Now let me go."

Octo-Cat held on for another few seconds to really get his point across, then released her.

"I'm sorry for the things we did," she recited tonelessly.

"Which was what exactly?" I asked, even though I already had an idea.

"We created a scene," she began with a bored expression, then smiled as she delved deeper. "And locked you in the room. And stole the rings. And ruined the dress."

Hearing her confirm my newly formed suspicions really twisted my gut. I'd blamed Pringle for things he had no part in. I'd forbidden him from sharing in the most important day of my life. I'd treated him like a criminal, even though he'd done nothing wrong.

Instead of asking *why*—Jacques had already explained that, after all—I wanted to know, "How?"

"There was a key in the door," Jacques

answered. "Jillianne gave me a boost, and I was able to turn it with my sphyngers before I fell back down."

Sphyngers. Huh. Now that these two were actually talking to me, it seemed I'd have a whole new lingo to learn.

"That lady who was supposed to be watching us yesterday was pretty distracted. It was easy for us to slip in and out without her noticing us," Jillianne added, apparently enjoying the villain's speech portion of their apology. "The rings were easy to nab from the top of the dresser and hide in our blanket. And we saw you let the raccoon in and listened when you told him it was okay if he was invited. We also saw how annoyed you were with him and figured it would be easy to frame him. So we invited him back inside right after we ruined the dress."

"That was a horrible thing to do!" I shouted, then remembered that I needed to keep quiet if I wanted to avoid inviting more company into this room before we finished our conversation.

"We're sorry," Jacques said again and rubbed against my arm. "We'll be good now."

Jillianne rolled her eyes but offered no verbal argument.

"I appreciate you sharing all this with me. And your apologies, too." I paused and chewed on my bottom lip. "But are we done here? There's someone I really need to apologize to."

"Good kitties," Octo-Cat said with a sage nod. "Now that you've done as promised, I'll keep up my end of the bargain. Let me show you where to get the fish."

I opened the door where Grizabella sat waiting in the hall.

The sphynxes ran out of the room and down the stairs, meowing excitedly the whole way, but Octo-Cat hung back.

"Thank you for that," I whispered.

He nodded again. "We still need to have that serious discussion about our future," the tabby told me.

I sucked in a deep breath, hating to do anything to ruin his big day when he'd done so much to save mine. But a reverse neuter simply wasn't possible. That wasn't something I could magically change, unfortunately.

Before I could say anything, Octo-Cat continued. "We need to have that talk, but it can wait. Grizabella and I have the rest of our nine lives together, and so do you and I, Angela. We'll talk when you get back. Now enjoy your honeymoon, okay?"

Once again, I cried big weeping tears of joy. I was really becoming quite the softie these days, but that's just what happened when a person was well and truly happy with their life.

20

"Cover for me while I pay Pringle a quick visit in his treehouse," I pleaded with Mags, knowing she hated the attention of the TV crew but unable to think of another way to get the privacy I needed when going to speak with the raccoon—and hopefully make amends while I was at it.

She reluctantly agreed, and I took off power-walking as stealthily as I could.

I found Pringle sitting in his primary tree house —he had two, after all—with his head pressed into the corner where two walls came together.

"Pringle?" I whispered as I finished climbing the ladder and situated myself on the wooden floor.

He wouldn't even turn to look at me, but at least

he was willing to talk. "I was bad. I'm sorry. I ruined the day, and I hurt you. I hurt my very best friend."

My heart broke for him. I'd been so sure he was helping Alpha sabotage my big day that I'd inadvertently sabotaged it myself. I'd closed off someone I love, and now I would never get the chance to include him in the memory of our ceremony. I did have a chance to do something special with him now though—just the two of us.

"I'm your best friend, huh?" I asked with a smile as I crossed my legs beneath my billowy gown.

"Of course you're my best friend," he practically exploded as he finally turned around to face me. "You do so much nice stuff for me. You got me my tree houses and my TV and Carla and everything. We always have so much fun together, even though sometimes I spoil things by being a bad raccoon."

I shook my head sadly. I'm the one who brought him to this point—me and only me. "You're not a bad raccoon, but I've been a bad friend. I'm sorry. Somehow I got it into my head that Alpha was using you to get to me. When he helped you join AA so soon after threatening to ruin the wedding, I was certain that you were a big part of his evil plan."

Pringle crept out of his corner on all fours and tilted his head in question. "Who's Alpha? I don't know any Alpha."

"You specifically told me, by name, that Alpha had suggested you join AA. Don't you remember?"

"Oh, I must have misspoken then. It wasn't Alpha, but it was a guy with a military-type name. You know the one who always comes around with his daughter, Abigull? Remember how I rescued her and saved the day? That was one of my great moments." He stared into the distance, as if remembering fondly.

"You've had a lot of great moments," I told him, unable to believe what he was revealing to me now. "But back up a sec. Are you saying it was Bravo who helped you? Not Alpha?"

"Yeah, I don't know an Alpha. Or, oh wait! Was he the guy who killed all of Abigull's flock? If so, that dude is bad news! He's definitely not allowed in our yard. If I saw him, I would chase him off or —or I'd shoot at him with Carla!" Carla was his Nerf gun that he used for causing trouble more than anything else. It probably wouldn't hold up as an actual weapon, but I did like that he was trying to look out for me. Still, I couldn't believe that all my paranoia and cold-shouldering had been because of a simple confusion over names. I should have known better, and I should have trusted both Pringle and Nan when they told me he wasn't to blame.

"Can you ever forgive me, Pringle?" I asked, unsure whether I actually deserved a fresh chance with him.

"Of course I forgive you!" the raccoon shouted happily, rising to his hind legs. "I was never mad. Just my feelings were hurt is all. I really thought we weren't best friends anymore."

I reached out my fist, and the raccoon bumped it with his much smaller hand. "We're still besties. Maybe one of these days you can tell me more about your twelve-step program and how you're making amends. Seems I could take a page or two from your book, Mr. Pringle."

He jumped up and then scampered to the other corner of his fort. "Which book? I found this one in the trash a couple weeks ago!" He waved a copy of a book with a cat on the cover called *Merlin takes a Familiar.* "Seriously, I don't know who would throw this beauty away. Look at this awesome cover! You can borrow it if you want."

"Haha, thanks," I said, accepting the paperback. I wasn't sure how much time I'd have to read on my honeymoon, but I could always read it after. Then I got an even better idea. "What if I read it to you so we can enjoy the story together?"

Pringle steepled his fingers and looked up at me with what could only be described as puppy-dog eyes. "Really? You would read it to me?"

"Of course. It doesn't look like the chapters are very long, so we can start right now with the first one if you're ready."

His pointed smile widened, but he shook his head. "No, not right now. It's your big day. Besides, you still have to open my present!"

"Your pres—" I stopped short. "I think I saw it on the gift table. It was the one wrapped in tra—um, in newspaper, right?"

He pointed at me and nodded. "Right-O. So what do you think? Can you open it right now?"

"There are a lot of people around who shouldn't know that you and I can talk. It could put us in danger, but if you want, you can tell me what it is," I suggested. The last gift Pringle had given me was a diamond ring, so really this could be anything.

He jumped up and down with excitement.

"Good, because I can't wait any longer. It's been so hard keeping this a secret from you, bestie!"

I laughed at his enthusiasm. It felt good to be here with him and put all my doubts and worries behind me. I'd been so mean to him, and yet he harbored no ill will. All he'd wanted was my approval. Animals were better than us in that regard.

"Tell me," I prompted, knowing I'd love whatever he'd gotten for me since it had truly come from his furry little heart.

"It's my namesake," he exclaimed.

I kept my expression neutral as I tried to puzzle it out. "A can of Pringles?" I guessed.

"Not just *a* can of Pringles, *the* can of Pringles. I was pretty much born in that can. My mother had just fished it out of the trash when she felt me and my two sisters getting ready to be born. She took the can and ran into the woods, but she didn't make it to the den in time. She had us right then and there, and then she packed us into this baby and carried us back to our home, safe and sound."

"Pringle," I gasped. "That's a beautiful story. But are you sure you want to give me something so important?"

"Surer than sure," he agreed. "My mom might

not be here anymore, but the day after she and my sisters were hit by that speeding car, I found the hole under your porch and moved in. I was so sad missing them, but then I met you, and my life got happy again."

"I'm glad you found that hole under my porch," I said tearfully, both from the kindness of this gesture and the tragedy of his backstory. I'd never heard it before, but now that I knew about his past, I thought I understood him a little better than before. And I definitely knew I could try harder to live up to the lofty title he'd entrusted to me.

Best friend.

EPILOGUE

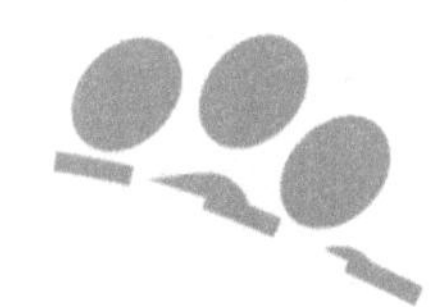

woke up the next morning floating on a cloud. A lady doesn't tell, but let's just say the wedding night more than lived up to expectations.

I was more in love with my husband than ever and couldn't wait to spend the next ten days with him, free of work and family obligations as we kicked off our new life together.

We'd spent last night in his house so we could have some privacy, but I wanted to swing back and say goodbye to everyone at my place before we officially took off.

Everyone was up and waiting, eager to show me all the wonderful photos they'd snapped the day before. I looked forward to seeing them, but it would have to be later. At least ten days later.

"I love you," I told the group that comprised Nan, Grant, Grandma Lyn, Mom, Dad, Mags, Sharon, and Christine, plus five mostly happy cats and one very excited little dog. "But we'll have to catch up once I'm back. Bye!"

Charles picked me up in his arms and carried me over the threshold—albeit moving in the wrong direction of what tradition dictated, the goof. He delivered me to the passenger side of his car and opened the door with a sweeping, knightly gesture. "My lady."

I giggled as I clicked my seatbelt into place.

My husband started up the car, and everyone gathered on the porch to wave. Nan even waved Paisley's little paw for her. Best of all, I could see Pringle hiding just around the side of the house, jumping up and down and waving with both arms.

"Shall we, Mrs. Longfellow?" my husband asked from beside me, a huge grin gleaming on his handsome face.

"We shall, Mr. Longf—Aaaaah!" I shouted in surprise as a giant blob of white hit the windshield right in front of me.

I unbuckled myself, opened the door, and bolted

out just in time to see a flash of white flying over the house. "Hahaha," Alpha cawed in victory as he moved out of sight. "Nailed it!"

Well, poop.

It looked like he'd gotten his revenge, after all.

Ready to find out new mysteries away Angie and Charles on their honeymoon? There are only two books left in the series. Make sure you don't miss a single adventure!

Get your copy of *Honeymoon Hearsay,* so that you can keep reading this series today!

Pssst… If you absolutely loved this book and want even more, make sure you **sign up for Molly's newsletter**. When you do, you'll receive an exclusive digital prize pack, including a free book!

WHAT'S NEXT?

The old stone mansion Charles and I have booked for our week-long honeymoon seems to be something straight out of a fairytale.

That is, until it all starts to fall apart. *Quite literally.* My poor husband plunges straight through the staircase on our first night--and it's a real wonder he didn't need serious medical intervention after that.

I want to find another place to stay, but Charles insists he's okay and that he'd like to see the week out. Of course, we become stucker than stuck when we stumble upon a lost kitten crying for her missing mama in the back garden.

We can't just leave her, but we also can't stay here, especially once deadly rumors begin buzzing in the garden... What happened to Charles wasn't a mistake, but he also may not be the intended target.

Time to find the kitten's mama and skedaddle. I just got married; I'm definitely not ready to become a widow!

HONEYMOON HEARSAY is now available.

Get your copy so that you can keep reading this zany mystery series today!

My name is Angie Longfellow. Yup, it's official as of the day before yesterday. I'm a married woman, who is currently headed toward a luxury honeymoon destination with new hubby at her side.

I still can't believe it really happened.

Getting married is probably the most normal thing I've done with my life, yet it also feels like the biggest adventure so far.

And that's saying something, considering I racked up seven associate degrees as I struggled with academic indecision, started my own business as a private investigator, and can secretly talk to animals.

Oh, you're wondering about that last part? Well, allow me to explain…

It all started with a will reading at the law firm where I used to work as a paralegal. The same law firm where I met my new husband—*eep!*—but I digress.

As a glorified secretary, it was my job to make the coffee. The partners hadn't sprung for new appliances in quite some time, and the coffee maker was more than a little worse for wear. When I tried to plug it in, the darned thing zapped me unconscious.

I woke up a short bit later to the smell of tuna and the sound of someone addressing me in a very condescending manner. I didn't know it then, but that someone was the deceased's beloved cat Octavius. He told me his owner had been murdered and that he needed help to prove it and thus get justice for the old lady he'd loved so dearly.

If you know cats as well as I do, then you know that Mr. Octavius refused to take "no" for an answer. With no choice but to comply, a partnership was born.

We solved the murder together and became friends while doing it. I was asked to adopt him by the estate's trustee, and I eagerly agreed—even before I knew a certain tabby had a generous trust fund attached to him.

I took to calling him Octo-Cat, and together we moved into his former owner's enormous manor house at his behest. Now the two of us are partners in crime… make that partners in *solving crimes.* Yes, we run the P.I. business together. We don't always agree, but one way or another, we always get the job done.

And it's because of my strange ability to speak with animals that I really got to know my new husband, Charles. He overheard me trying to sneak in a FaceTime call with Octo-Cat at work—and proceeded to use this knowledge to blackmail me into helping with a difficult case he'd just landed.

That all worked out too, even though honestly he could have just politely asked for my help rather than resorting to blackmail. I already had a huge crush on him and would have jumped at any excuse to spend more time together. And time is all we have on our lengthy two-day drive from Maine to Virginia.

My mom and dad managed to book a gorgeous private mansion for our honeymoon, and we'll have the entire place to ourselves for a whole week to usher in our era of newly wedded bliss. It's the same place they honeymooned more than thirty years ago, which bodes well for us, seeing as the two of them are still crazy in love.

I'll miss everyone while we're away for the week, but I know Nan will keep everyone back home in check. Lucky for her, she won't be able to understand all the complaints Octo-Cat and Charles's two hairless cats, Jacques and Jillianne, are sure to send her way. She'll also have her sweet rescue dog Paisley to keep her company and her brand-new surprise husband Grant, along with his Holland Lop bunny EB. It's a full house for sure!

I'm sure I'll still call at least once per day to play translator and mediator for whatever problems arise, but it's nothing my scrappy grandmother can't handle... Provided our resident raccoon Pringle behaves himself. Lately he's been turning over a new leaf with the help of a certain twelve-step program, and we recently shared a very heart-felt bonding moment, but his natural tendencies still encourage him to gossip and thieve whenever possible.

But no, I'm sure it will all be fine—just fine.

I need to stop worrying about everyone we left in Maine and focus on the wonderful week in Virginia ahead. It's my honeymoon, and my new husband deserves my full attention. It will probably be good for me to have this little break from all the drama and chaos of the busy household back home. I can put out any fires when I return next week.

This week is all about celebrating my new marriage, and that's exactly what I plan to focus on.

* * *

"Look at the trees," I remarked, pointing out the side window as Charles and I entered the final hour of our big road trip. We were getting very close to the old stone mansion where we'd be spending the next week, and I was jittery with excitement. "They're changing."

"We've got a long way until autumn," he answered while fiddling with the radio.

I shook my head and pointed again. "No, like they're a completely different type. We don't have trees like this back in Blueberry Bay."

"Touché." He laughed. "Leave it to you to notice the forest *and* the trees."

"You can take the detective out of the agency..." I laughed too. "But no sleuthing this week. Promise."

I grabbed Charles's hand from the radio while he used the other to guide the steering wheel. "The next seven days are about you and me, and only you and me."

"I like the sound of that," he said flirtatiously before raising our linked hands to kiss the back of mine. "And we're almost there. Our turn-off is in less than thirty miles, and from there it's a straight shot to our little Southern slice of paradise."

"So what should we do first once we get there?"

"Oh, I think you know, Mrs. Longfellow." He glanced toward me for a second, then winked before returning his gaze to the highway.

Heat rushed to my cheeks. I was still very new at being a wife and not yet comfortable with all the intricacies that came with the role. Especially with talking about them.

So I redirected the conversation a little bit. "I mean, *after*? I've been reading about the area on Trip Advisor. There are all kinds of historical tours, and some really nice restaurants, and..."

Charles squeezed my hand. "This is our honeymoon. It's not about seeing the sights. Let's just relax and enjoy each other's company."

I wriggled in my seat. "Relax, right. I can do that."

He chuckled good-naturedly. "Yes, you can. If your workaholic husband can enjoy some time off the grid, then so can you. Besides, we'll have each other, and that's all we really need, right?"

"Right," I said, nodding my head sharply, which only sent us both into another fit of giggles. "This week is only about us, but we can still try some of the local restaurants, right? I might die if I don't get true authentic Southern-made biscuits and gravy for breakfast at least once this week."

"Of course! We'll have them every day if you'd like. We'll need something to keep up our stamina between... well, you know."

I blushed like mad at the implication and tried to hide my hot cheeks behind my palms.

"Oh, Angie Longfellow, I love you. Never change," my husband said before releasing my hand to casually rub my shoulder.

Never change. Now that I could do. But could I avoid all my usual worries and busy-bodying for one whole week?

I guess time would tell on that one.

HONEYMOON HEARSAY is now available.

**Get your copy so that you can keep reading
this zany mystery series today!**

ABOUT MOLLY FITZ

While *USA Today bestselling* author Molly Fitz can't technically talk to animals, she and her three feline writing assistants have deep and very animated conversations as they navigate their days.

She lives with her child and their own private zoo somewhere in the wilds of Alaska. Molly will occasionally venture out for good food, great coffee, or to meet new animal friends.

Learn more about Molly and her books, and be sure to sign up for her newsletter at **www.Molly Mysteries.com**.

ALSO BY MOLLY FITZ

Learn more about Molly's collected works, so that you can decide which book you'd like to read next...

PET WHISPERER P.I.

Angie Russo just partnered up with Blueberry Bay's first ever talking cat detective. Along with his ragtag gang of human and animal helpers, Octo-Cat is determined to save the day... so long as it doesn't interfere with his schedule.

Start with book 1, ***Kitty Confidential***.

MERLIN'S MAGICAL MYSTERIES

Gracie Springs is not a witch... but her cat is. Now she must help to keep his secret or risk spending the rest of her life in some magical prison. Too bad trouble seems to find them at every turn!

Start with book 1, ***Merlin Takes a Familiar***.

PARANORMAL TEMP AGENCY

Tawny Bigford's simple life takes a turn for the magical when she stumbles upon her landlady's murder and is recruited by a talking black cat named Fluffikins to take over the deceased's role as the official Town Witch for Beech Grove, Georgia.

Start with book 1, ***Witch for Hire***.

THE MYSTERIES OF MOONLIGHT MANOR (WITH TRIXIE SILVERTALE)

Sydney Coleman has it all—until she doesn't. No sooner does she launch her bed and breakfast, than a trio of ghosts turn up oppose her at every turn. They insist she solve the murder of their mistress, but Sydney is desperate for cash. If she can't book some guests fast, her haunted mansion is utterly doomed.

Start with book 1, **Moonlight & Mischief**.

CONNECT WITH MOLLY

Sign up for my newsletter and get a special digital prize pack for joining, including an exclusive story, *Meowy Christmas Mayhem*, fun quiz, and lots of cat pictures!

Sign up: **MollyMysteries.com/subscribe**

Now, if you ever wished you could converse with cats, here's your opportunity! This is me officially inviting you into my whacky inner world as part of my Cozy Kitty Book Club.

For those who just can't get enough of my zany cat characters and their hapless humans, this book club will provide new content to devour and the chance to get to know my best author friends.

From exclusive stories, behind-the-scenes trivia to never-before-released bonus content, and monthly giveaways, there's a lot to love about the Cozy Kitty Book Club. Join today to find out what we're reading next!

Join: **MollyMysteries.com/club**

9 781644 515266